GRAYSON

Grayson

The Lycan Knights

K. L. STEPHENS

Karen L. Stephens

Copyright

Dedication

For my brother Tymm, I miss you every day. But I know you are looking down and reading over my shoulder as I write. Even whispering into the cosmos ideas.

I will love and miss you until we meet again.

Synopsis

A TREASURE HUNT - MURDER - SECRETS ARE
REVEALED

Author K. L. Stephens had brought another steamy paranormal romance to life. Grayson is the third book in the Lycan Knights paranormal romance series where the Templar's Treasure is in danger of being found.

Treasure hunters are getting closer than before to finding The Templar's treasure. Only one clue remains hidden inside the ruins of Sinclair castle, and Grayson has gone with one of his Knights of Arcadia brothers, to retrieve it.

When Grayson finds his mate precariously climbing up the side of the castle ruins, he comes to her aid, only to release she is one of the treasure hunters getting close to discovering what they have been hiding for centuries.
He is determined to keep his mate safe from herself but all the other deadly treasures hunters that are hot on her trail.

Contents

Prologue

Woods Outside Sinclair Castle, Wick Scotland
1680

Ewan Sinclair

I stood several feet from the edge of the tree line, far enough back that the humans could not see me. The treasure was hidden in a cave some one hundred and fifty feet over the cliff of Sinclair castle; only our families knew it was there. The human Clans of Campbell and Sinclair were fighting over this land and title. I had not dared to get closer. At the sound of someone approaching, my eyes glowed red, and my stance was ready for an attack. Instead of a human soldier, I turned to greet my old friend, Andris Meyer.

We embraced as brothers, pointing to the castle. "I think we need to get the treasure away from this place," I stated.

"And the clue?" Andris asked, nodding his eyes glowed as he scanned the area looking at all the ongoing activity.

Next, I pointed to a window, "It is hidden in the sill of that tower window, there on the third floor. Humans will not risk climbing up there since that explosion destroyed it years ago. They have not yet tried to rebuild it." I added. "With all these humans around, I think it would be too risky for us to try to get the clue without being seen." We watched the activity around the castle grounds for a few minutes when I added.

"The humans have been bringing in cannons and ammunition over the last few days. This battle could start any time; we need to move the treasure as soon as possible," I advised.

We watched the humans as they scrambled to put their cannons in place for the impending battle. Andris nodded and asked, "When do the others get here?"

"Naeem is the furthest. I sent the message to him first so that I would say within another day or so," responded. "We can stay on our lands."

Andris nodded in agreement and slapped me on the back, smiling, as he inquired, "How is your family?"

Grinning, "My Grayson, like your Levi is training to be a knight with the order. And my Murdoc is strong and will make a fine clan leader." Chuckling, "He is eager to mate and sniffs around any female he gets near." Laughing, we joked as we remembered when we were young and sniffed around all the females that came near us. We turned and walked back further into the woods, where we had horses tethered to a tree, then rode to the Lycan Sinclair keep.

Over the next week, the rest of my friends and brothers-in-arms arrived. Then we finalized our plans. On the appointed night after dark, Andris and Naeem rowed two boats around the cove as three of us climbed down the side of the cliff to the cave. Liam stayed on top, to lower the picks and shovels we would need then untied the ropes so one of my brothers could catch them. Then we would use them to lower the treasure down to Andris and Naeem. Our plan worked without a hitch, and we were able to get the treasure unseen to the Sinclair Lycan compound.

Now that the treasure was safely back in our control, we could breathe some relief. Over the following weeks, we packed up our mates and our youngest children. Then just as our fathers traveled through Europe, we traveled in covered wagons east across Scotland to Ayr. We boarded a ship bound for Canada, as many Scottish humans have done since the Jacobite uprising. The 'New World,' as the humans called it, was a safe place to establish a new compound with our mates and young and hide the treasure once again.

After we secured land that we could build on, I sent a letter to my son Grayson, informing him of our location and telling him where the clue was hidden in Sinclair Castle, for now, the clue and treasure are safe.

Chapter 1

Cave Deep in the Black Forest, Germany
1785

Jacob Maxwell

"Have you found it yet?" My long-time classmate from Oxford called out from behind where I was digging.

"Shhh! I am digging." I harshly whispered back. "Be quiet; this whole cave could come down on us, with the slightest sound or vibration," I warned him, wondering *why I even told him about my search for the Templar's treasure and this possible clue hidden here.* Then I remembered his father was wealthy and funded this little excursion of mine. His father thought this was all his son's idea to find this body. So, he funded our trip. I could hear my friend scooting closer and holding on to my pants leg. "Stop right there! You won't fit up here with me; I barely fit." Turning, I could see his disappointment written all over his face.

"Then change places with me." He whispered back. Just then, my fingers fell on the skeletal bones of a hand. I turned my attention to what I found, the hand was clutching the remnants of a leather cylinder, and surprisingly it was still intact. I had ignored my friend's plea to come closer. I pried the cylinder free; I didn't care about the ancient remains of the man, just the cylinder and its contents. As I turned it around to examine the cylinder, it was just as I was read in a long-ago journal, the seal on the top was that of Pope Celestine V. My heart was racing, this was it, this was the clue to the Templar's treasure. I found it!

I had not been paying attention to my friend in all my excitement until his hand reached out and snatched the cylinder from mine. "We found it!" he exclaimed. "We are going to be rich beyond anything!"

Fury that I have never known before welled up inside me, what did he mean by 'WE'? My hand reached out, and instead of snatching back the cylinder, my fingers grasped a rock. Then as if I was watching someone else's hand, I struck his head not once, but at least five times. He was dead, no longer recognizable, one of his eyes had disappeared into the indent from the repeated impact of the rock in his skull, and the other eye was open and looked at me in shock. As I had struck him, blood had sprayed out all over my chest and face and more still poured from his gaping mouth. I killed him, and I was not sorry for it. I was the one that did all the research and found the old journal. I spent countless hours translating Latin, and all he did was get his father to fund this trip. No, this was my treasure, not his.

When I returned to my senses, I realized I needed to cover up what I had done. I took the cylinder and carefully placed it in my backpack. Searching my now-dead friend's pockets for his money pouch and then secured it also in my backpack, not even bothering to count what was there yet. I scooted back away from him and the skeleton, pulling out the braces we had placed to hold up the roof over where we were digging.

Dirt and rocks started to fall as I retreated closer to the cave opening. When I was far enough back, I pulled the last main brace and watched as the cave collapsed on top of him, burying him with at least a ton of rock and dirt with the skeleton, thankfully no part of him was visible. Before I exited the cave, I found another rock and struck my head, blood trickled down my face. I rubbed dirt on my face and tore open my shirt and pants. I just hoped that I looked like I barely made it out of the cave myself.

After I hid my backpack safely away from the cave opening, I limped my way back to the little village we had been staying in. My voice trembled and I stared wide-eyed, relaying the story I had come up with on my walk back to the village. I told them my friend and I were in a cave, and it collapsed, my friend didn't make it out, and I feared for him. In the back of my head, I thought I could have been an actor on stage, I did such a convincing job. Men from the village came to try to dig him out, and some of the women cleaned and dressed the wound on my head. After several hours, the sun was beginning to set so, the villagers proclaimed they could not proceed any further for fear of getting caught in another collapse, there was just too much dirt and rock, and it was unstable. Thank God no one saw the relief I felt that his body would probably never be recovered. At least not in my lifetime.

That night I sat at the small writing desk in the room of the inn my friend and I had shared, composing a letter to his father. I told him about the terrible accident, and that his son had died. I mentioned that the villagers had come to try to dig him out, but there was just too much earth to move. And unfortunately, we were unsuccessful in finding our clue before the collapse. Nearly escaping with my own life, I was giving up the search. I thought that was a nice touch. After I finished,

I found the rest of my friend's money from his father and packed my bags. Just before sunrise, I returned and retrieved my backpack, to the inn before the innkeeper had stirred. After a nice big breakfast, I left. With the money I retrieved from my friend's body and belongings, I had enough to leave for good. The semester ended before we came to Germany, and I didn't need to return to Oxford. So, I headed home back to the United States, California to be exact. The civil war was over, and I could start a new life and continue my treasure hunt.

Chapter 2

Stamford University, California
Present Day

Samantha

After spending the night at the campus library, my eyes were blurry and my head was pounding, but I found what I was looking for, the next clue. It had been right there, for years and no one had found it, taking a deep breath, I had to calm down. Closing my research notebooks, and laptop, I ran to my small apartment just off campus. After I got out of the shower, I opened my laptop and found the flights I needed to get to Scotland, even with the cheapest airfare, I was still going to max out my credit cards, and probably empty my savings account, but if I could find it, all of the struggles will be well worth it. I was headed to Edinburgh, Scotland. There was a Seventeenth-century journal located in the library of Edinburgh University. Once I find it, I would know where to go next. My heart was racing; I found the clue that the Professor had been searching for all his life.

Not just the professor, if he was to be believed, it all started back with his ancestor in the mid to late seventeen hundreds. The professor had refused to let me read his ancestor's diaries, nor would he let me see the document he spoke about with reverence. The document his ancestor had dug up. But it didn't matter, he had infected me with the treasure-hunting bug, and I was hooked.

Looking at the time on my screen, I closed up everything and walked to Professor Maxwell's office. Arriving before him, I was sitting in the reception area tapping my foot nervously as I waited for him. As soon as he stepped off the elevator, I blurted out, "I found the next clue!"

As soon as he was arm's length away, he grabbed my arm and nearly shoved me through his office door closing it with a thud behind him. "Samantha, slow down. And quietly tell me what you are talking about." He demanded to know.

For a small man, his grip on my arm was strong, rubbing where his fingers had dug in, I was so preoccupied with my excitement that I hardly noticed the pain. Nor did I note the intent in his eyes. I explained that I read about the journal that is now housed in the Edinburgh library, which could lead me to the treasure's location. It was somewhere in Scotland, how it got there from Jerusalem was beyond me, but there it was. Further, I explained I had already booked my flight for Scotland and would be leaving tomorrow, I just needed to pack up a few things and go see my father before I left.

The professor sat behind his desk listening and making notes as I spoke. Continuing to ramble on my thoughts, this would be a great ending to my master's thesis if I could find the treasure. And I could support my father for the rest of his life. I owed him that much. As I blathered, I missed the professor's scowl at the last statement.

After I left the professor's office, I walked home, calming down. This was it; I knew it. When I got home, I packed up what I needed in clothes, including my research notebooks and laptop putting them all in my backpack. Then I left and took a bus to my father's. I didn't have a car, and I would spend the night there. I had no worries that he would drive me to the airport tomorrow.

We had a pleasant evening and talked about me finding the treasure. "I am so close dad; I can feel it," I said with excitement.

He kissed my forehead and nodded. "I know you will find it, my love." My father never doubted me or questioned my obsession with finding the treasure.

There was a worried look on his face, "What is it?" I asked.

"I just wonder how the professor is going to feel when you are the one that finds the treasure." He mused. "I don't think he is going to like it." The last was a mumble, and he realized I was not paying attention, my mind was racing.

Shrugging my shoulders I spoke, "I told you I felt he had been having his students do all the research for some years." Then I looked out the window, "I am not going to give it to him just for a good grade, dad." My voice was stern.

Realizing I had heard him he stood from his seat came over and hugged me, "I am not worried about your grades, I am worried about you, Torie. Please just be careful." I went to bed soon after but was just as determined in the morning.

The flight to Scotland was thirteen hours long, and I had booked a quaint inn not far from Edinburgh University, part of their service was to pick me up from the airport. Which I appreciated, being somewhere I had never been. The driver chatted away in Gaelic, which I only caught a word or two, but I continued to smile and nod as he drove.

My room was cozy, and the bed was comfortable, thinking I was the only one that would be looking for the journal, I took the next day to get some sleep and recover from jetlag. On the following morning, I walked over to the library and got permission to look at the ancient book. Explaining I was doing research for my thesis. The librarian graciously took me to a table and brought the journal to me, handing me white gloves. Doing as I was instructed, I now had white-gloved hands so I could gingerly turn pages until I found what I was looking for. I opened my notebook, and made the necessary notes, about where I would be going and what I would be looking for. Even though it was all in Gaelic, I used my translator on my phone and took pictures of the pages I needed.

Before I could close the book, I saw a warning, it said *fear - madadh-allaidh*. For some reason this stood out to me, entering the words in my translator and found out it meant man-wolf. Why would there be a warning about a wolf I wondered? Shaking my head, thinking this was just some superstition to ward people off, I put the thought out of my head, thanking the staff, as I walked out of the library. I only needed to spend one more night at the inn, tomorrow morning I would need to find the bus station; I was headed to Wick, Scotland more precisely Sinclair Castle. I was determined to find the Templar's treasure.

Chapter 3

Highlands of Scotland

Grayson

Breathing deeply, it felt good to be back in the highlands. The landscape had changed in the last three hundred years, but the smells of heather, lavender, and smoky peat filled the air, making me feel like my old self again. I left this part of the world years ago to train with the order. Like my grandfather, and father, I was a knight of the Order of Arcadia. It was the same for my five friends; we were all destined to be knights from birth. And being the descendants of the original six that hid the treasure, we were now responsible to make sure that it remained hidden.

A copy of the 1293 death warrant from Pope Celestine V resurfaced some ten years ago when Samantha was kidnapped by her uncle. The same death warrant was found back in the late 1700s by some archaeology students in Germany. Our grandfathers were named in the warrant as was the Templar's treasure. So, it was decided it was time to get the remaining clue hidden by our fathers out of Scotland.

Noah and I spent the night sleeping near Loch Fleet. Getting up early, we were on our Harleys' traveling northeast to

Wick. My stomach growled, "I miss Samantha's cooking," I grumbled more to myself than Noah.

Chuckling: "Yeah, you're not a gourmet." Noah agreed, rubbing his empty stomach as it grumbled too. We had seen Lucas and Samantha off from her father's private airport three nights ago, they were headed home. Now we are traveling to Castle Sinclair outside Wick located in the farthest northeastern part of the Highlands.

The castle was in ruins now, but our fathers had hidden a clue in the castle while it was being built in the 1480s. Levi had heard through his numerous contacts around the world that treasure hunters looking for the treasure and may be getting close. And then there was Tavish, the mysterious assistant that helped with Samantha's kidnapping. There was no choice, we had to retrieve it. The Templar's treasure was left to us to protect with our lives if needed, just as it had been by our grandfathers.

Spotting a fueling station and tavern up ahead, we pulled over. Noah opened the door, but I had to duck through the doorway to the tavern. Even in my human form, my six-foot-seven height was taller than most door frames. Heads turned to gawk at me as we walked in looking to find a place to sit. We found an empty table in the back corner where we could keep our backs to the wall and our eyes on the humans coming and going.

A waitress came up and asked for our order, she was nervous, and her eyes kept darting from her order pad to me. I was used to humans being uncomfortable around me, so I smiled and ordered meals in Gaelic. "It must be my good looks that have her so nervous." Noah boasted.

Looking around, I spotted some hikers, asking for directions to Sinclair castle. Another waitress pulled out a map, that the owners had under a glass counter to sell to tourists, showing them the way. "We may have some company," I said quietly to Noah, motioning toward the hikers. I was pretty sure they were not the treasure hunters that we were watching out for. And we had a vague idea of what Tavish looked like from Levi's search. He was a master at disguising himself, we found several different pictures of him, each just a little bit different than the last.

As we watch, it was apparent that these humans looked more like simple tourists, and we were not here to make trouble, but I learned over the centuries to always be prepared for it. We had one job to do, and we could quickly get it done at dusk.

After eating we headed to the castle. We were close to my family holdings, but we didn't stop. We had a task to complete, and once we arrived, we parked our bikes out of site. The clue was hidden in the third-floor windowsill of the tower, and with the castle, in ruins, we would have to climb. We put on Sinclair kilts, they were loose and easier to climb in, rather than tight-fitting pants. We choose the darker of the Sinclair tartan colors, not the bright red and green so that we would not be seen in the coming darkness. Dusk was upon us, walking around to the side of the building inspecting and looking for the best route up. Since we had passed the hikers hours ago, along the side of the road, I didn't think that they would get here until tomorrow.

Looking around, it was sad to see the castle in the shape it was in now. There had been an explosion in the 1600s that destroyed it, and humans have never sought to rebuild. From what we knew, there were still disputes and court cases regarding this land and title. Just as we moved to the main part of what remained of the five-story tower building, I inhaled to catch the scent of the seawater that crashed on the rocks two hundred feet below, but something more filled the air, a stirring filled me, and my beast reacted to her smell. My Mate! Turning my head looked up then over to Noah, "She's here."

Noah looked over, "WHAT? Now?" He asked with a disbelieving tone, then shaking his head, he slapped me on the back, "Congratulations, but we still have a job to do." We both then looked up, there she was about forty feet above us on the side of the ruins!

I agreed, "Who is she talking to?" I whispered, then Noah looked up again to where she was barely hanging on to the rocks that comprised the shell of the castle talking to herself.

"This is a mess you have gotten yourself into, Vickie." She looked up and then around for a place to put her hand or foot. "You are going to die here and for what? Another wild goose chase! That's what! Those rock-climbing classes are nothing like the real thing." She didn't have a rope to hold her if she lost her grip, that two-hundred-foot drop to the water crashing on the rocks below would surely kill her.

Noah was watching her too, "She is going to kill herself." He whispered to me.

"Great, Now I am hearing voices" She grumbled, she had heard Noah but had not looked down and still had not seen us as she continued to talk to herself.

Shaking my head, I took a deep breath and started to climb. I was about three feet below and the left of her, when she turned her head and spotted me. Startled, she lost her grip. Reaching out, I caught her around her waist. "I've got you mo chara." I whispered as I pulled her close to my chest.

Her eyes were wide with fright. Abruptly twisting to look down to the water crashing below, she gulped then wrapped her arms around my neck nearly choking me, "Who's got you?" she cried out.

I inhaled and drew her scent into my core. Growling at the feel of her body next to mine. My beast stirred '*Claim her*'. She looked down, "Your chest just moved," she exclaimed.

Since we were hanging on the side of the ruins this was not the time or place to explain that she is mine forever. I had to get her down to safety. Looking over my shoulder, "You got her?" I called down to Noah a few feet below me.

"Aye." He answered.

"Take hold of my arm, we will get you down." Instructing, slowly one hand at a time she removed her grip from around my neck, once she had a firm grip on my arm, I lifted her down to Noah. It didn't take us long to get her back to solid ground.

When I was back on the ground as well, I took her hand and motioned to Noah to finish our task. She started to look up to watch Noah climb the side of the ruin. Bringing her face back to mine, "He doesn't have anything on under that kilt mo chara." I whispered with a grin.

Her eyes were the color of moss that covered the north side of the trees. Her hair was a rich walnut and long. It was pulled back away from her face in a braid that hung over her shoulder. The rest of her had my beast pacing, *"Ours!"*

She was watching me, "Your eyes just changed color?" Retreating a step from me, "What are you?" her voice trembled.

Before I could or would answer her question I asked one of my own, "What were you doing up there?" I softened my tone. She was already skittish, and I didn't want her to run. Besides she was backing up closer and closer to the edge of the cliff. Reaching out, I grasped her hand and pulled her forward stepping back as I went. For now, I would let her have her distance, soon enough she would learn the truth, that I would never let her go, she was mine.

She glanced over her shoulder and saw that I was moving her away from the danger of falling. "I was looking for something," she uttered, evading telling me the whole truth, I could tell by the way her eyes darted to the left and right, trying to avoid looking at mine.

I smiled, "Did you lose an earring up there?" teasing I chuckled out the question.

Subconsciously she checked to see if her earrings were in place. Then she giggled, "No, I was looking for a clue," answering me. Her voice was sweet as honey.

Noah whistled, "We have company coming." As he walked up from behind me, he signaled that he retrieved the clue and that it was safe.

"Where did he come from?" She asked, looking up at the ruins Noah had just climbed and then back at him.

"Gray?" Noah asked permission to speak to her. I nodded to him, "Our motorcycles we have parked over there." And he pointed in the direction of the bikes.

She looked around me to where he was pointing then cleared her throat, "I guess since you saved me, I should introduce my-self. I am Victoria Campbell; you may call me Vickie." She held out her hand, but her tone had turned formal, as she spoke.

Taking her hand again, "I am Grayson Sinclair, you may call me Gray. And this is Noah, a friend of mine." I turned when I heard the vehicles coming closer. "Where are you staying, Victoria?" I asked.

Noah had heard them as well and turned to head back to our bikes. "I was planning on camping out here." She watched as Noah disappeared. "Why?" she asked.

"Show me?" Then realizing that I needed to soften the re-quest, "Please." I didn't demand, but I was not about to let her stay here alone and unprotected.

She led me over to where she had thankfully just dropped her backpack. Picking it up, I tightened my grip on her hand, "We need to leave now Victoria," I said, this time not waiting for her to question or argue with me, I just pulled her along. My stride was longer than her shorter frame, she was running to keep up until I slowed my stride, "It isn't safe for you or us to stay here." I added, to let her know my reason for getting her away.

Walking into the building where our bikes were parked, I tossed her backpack to Noah, "Go! We will catch up with you in the morning." I barked, looking over my shoulder at the vehicles getting closer.

She watched in horror as Noah sped off with her belongings. "Hey, he has all my research!" she cried out horrified.

As I lifted her to the back of my Harley, she yelped, "Don't worry, he will give it back, when we meet up again," I reassured her, then swinging my leg over I climbed on my Harley in front of her tucking my kilt under me, "Wrap your arms around me." I ordered as I kickstarted my bike, I headed in the opposite direction as Noah.

"He went the other direction." She pointed out still horrified. I just nodded. She had no idea the trouble she had gotten herself into. I am pretty sure she was looking for the last piece of information that had been left in the castle by our fathers some six hundred years ago.

I turned off the headlight on my bike, I had no trouble seeing in the darkness. And I knew exactly where I was going. Placing my hand on top of hers clasped in front of me, "You are safe with me, mo chara." I called over my shoulder so she could hear me.

"You called me that before. I know *mo* means my or mine. What does *chara* mean?" She called out.

We were now in the dense forest, so I slowed down, "It means Mate." Calling over my shoulder again. I heard her as she gasped when I said, mate.

Chapter 4

Highlands of Scotland

Victoria

'Mate?' I must have heard him wrong, with the roar of the engine, trying to carry on a conversation was impossible. I will just have to wait until we stop to get to the bottom of this. But he didn't seem like he was going to stop any time soon. Even in the dark, I could see the trees flying past us as he weaved around them, sometimes coming so close I was surprised he had not crashed. But Grayson seemed to know exactly where he was going, at least that was my prayer, so I just closed my eyes and leaned my head on his back.

Grayson patted my hand and asked, "Did you fall asleep?" When I opened my eyes, I noticed that he had slowed down to a reasonable speed.

"No," I answered, "But the trees moving past us so fast was making me seasick and dizzy."

He patted my hand again, "Then just close your eyes, we will be stopping soon." His voice was laced with concern for my well-being, and it felt nice. Admittedly everything about him felt nice. I closed my eyes again, and inhaled, Grayson Sinclair, smelled like the woods, and was pure male.

When he had gotten me down to the ground, I was never more thankful. Just his sheer strength alone was amazing, he caught me and lifted me as if I weighed not more than a feather. And I knew that was not true. When I started college, I gained a little more than my freshman fifteen. Then after my parents divorced, I put on more weight. But when he looked at me, I didn't see the disgust I normally saw in men's eyes, I saw more. I just could not put my finger on it.

Grayson pulled up to a massive cave opening, and stopped, slowing I reopened my eyes, it was well hidden surrounded by dense woods all around. "We can camp here for the night." He said as he got off the bike and lifted me to the ground. I heard a low growl come from him as he slid me down the front of him.

Embarrassed I looked around, not sure what to do. Finally, I gave up, "Uhm, I need to?" I whispered mortified that I had to admit to him my problem.

Smiling Grayson pointed to the left, "There is a clearing about twenty yards that way." Turning he started to pick up pieces of wood, "Just call out if you get lost." He called over his shoulder. "I will hear you."

I scoffed at him. "Lost my ass. I will have you know I was a Girl Scout." My boast was short-lived, not twenty minutes later, I had turned to look this way then that I was not sure which way I needed to get back to the cave. I whispered. "Grayson."

He was standing right behind me, "You got lost, didn't you?" Chuckling as he reached for my hand, "Some Girl Scout you are."

Walking us back to the campsite he set up, there was a fire burning. I sat cross-legged in front of it holding out my hands to the fire. "Thank you for this."

He pulled what looked like a huge blanket from his bag and wrapped me in it. "This is my extra kilt. You should be warm in this."

It was soft well-worn wool and it smelled like him, "What about you? Won't you be cold?" I started to take it off to return it to him, but he stopped me.

Shaking his head, "I will be warm enough, stay covered up, it gets cold here at night. Now stay right there, I am going to go get us some dinner." As he was disappearing into the dense woods, he called over his shoulder, "If you need me just call out, I will hear you." Looking around I started to hum a song from my Girl Scout days, something about friends, gold, and silver. But I could not remember the words exactly. With every twig that snapped my humming got louder as my nervousness increased.

Grayson appeared about fifteen minutes later, carrying a branch with berries, a leather pouch, and a rabbit. At least that is what I think it was, he had taken the time to clean it. I watched with fascination as he created a spit to roast the rabbit over the fire. "Were you a Boy Scout or something?" I asked.

He had a nice laugh, "No, they don't have Boy Scouts this far up in Scotland." His head turned at the snap of a twig, inhaling he stood saying, "I will be right back." Then he walked off to the right into trees. This time curiosity got a hold of me, and I followed just to the edge of the trees. I could not see him or the person he was talking to but there was someone there. They were talking so fast I could not make out what they were saying, and I really didn't speak Gaelic all that well.

When I heard him coming back toward me, I ran back to the fire and turned the rabbit over the flames. As he sat down, "Were you talking to someone?" I asked with a blasé tone, not taking my eyes off the flames, I hoped that he thought the blush on my cheeks was from the fire and not me spying.

He tilted my face to look at him, "Yes, it was one of the sentries that are posted around this land." He was leaning up against a boulder, "You came to the edge of the trees but no further." He didn't show anger more humor that I had spied on him.

I gasped in shock that he knew, "I was quiet, how did you know?" I asked then realized I gave myself away with my admittance.

He was grinning at my boldness, and honesty, "I heard you, and I could see you." Leaning up he checked the rabbit, "And you let the rabbit burn on one side."

All I could do is shrug my shoulders, "I am sorry, I am a bit nosey at times. Do you know the people that own this land?" I wasn't sure my voice was contrite.

Grayson was still smiling at me, "This is my brother's land." He replied.

Again, I was shocked; "This is your home?" inquiring.

His gaze never left mine, "No, it is my brother's land. He is the head of our clan." Seeing that I was going to ask more, "I grew up here until I left for my training." He expanded his answer. Though I nodded that I understood, I really didn't, his answers were vague and that just brought up more and more questions.

It was his turn to ask a question, "What was the clue you were looking for back at the castle?"

That made me smile, I loved talking about my research. "There is supposed to be a clue to where the Templar treasure is hidden in one of the upper floors' windowsills."

"How did you know to look there?" he asked, something told me this was more than just curiosity and not just to keep our conversation going.

"There is an old journal in the library at Edinburgh University," I answered, he just nodded. Seeing that I was getting suspicious of his questions he changed the subject.

Crossing his arms over his massive chest, "You could have gotten yourself killed climbing up the side of that ruin you know that." His voice was full of concern, but his look was intent like he was instructing a child.

My defenses were up, "Why were you two there?" Then I remembered he said we were not safe there. "And why did you say we were not safe to stay there?" Another thought popped into my head. "And did you say I was your mate?"

His eyes flashed again as he smiled, "That is a lot of questions, Victoria." He said, "Which one do you want me to start with?" He looked relaxed with his back up against the boulder and his massive legs stretched out, then crossed at the ankles, his boots were rich leather and covered his calves, his arms were muscular, and folded across his chest, and the material of the sleeves of the t-shirt he wore stretched to the limit. With his kilt on he looked more like a highlander hero, I had read about in books. And. I could have sworn, that there was a small growl that came from him as my gaze went from his head to his feet.

Looking back at his face, I came back to the present, "The mate one, please." I said clearly.

Grayson nodded, "I did call you my mate because you are." It was a matter-of-fact statement.

Shaking my head, "Nope you are going to have to explain better than that." I was getting riled up, and he was grinning at me like a fool. "Why do you think I am your mate?" I asked again, like him I crossed my arms over my chest. Catching his eyes as the quickly looked at my breasts now pushed up further, but I had to get him to be clear on this subject.

"I don't think you are my mate; I know you are. But the simple answer is I caught your scent." He actually nodded like that statement should make all the scene to me in the world.

I shook my head, "You could smell me?" I asked with a nervous laugh, "That's crazy, of course, you could smell me. I can smell you too, but why do you think I am your mate?" I asked again exasperated. I didn't understand what he was thinking. It was just then I realized I had no idea where I was, and here alone in the middle of the woods somewhere in the Highlands with a complete stranger that keeps calling me his mate. *Way to stay safe, Vickie.* I thought looking around for a way to escape if I needed to.

Just as I turned to look for an escape, he uttered as if reading my mind. "I will never hurt you Victoria, I would die before I would let you get hurt." And I believed him, if I was being honest with myself, since he caught me when I lost my grip on the side of the castle, I have felt safe. I didn't understand why, but I did. But that didn't change the fact that he was a stranger, and I was in the middle of nowhere with him.

It was time to change the subject, "Why was it not safe for me or you to be at the castle?" He smiled again, "Are you laughing at me?"

He shook his head, "No, I am not laughing. You are tenacious, and I like it." He said, "There are treasure hunters also looking for the Templar treasure." His gaze was piercing, "They would stop at nothing to get to the treasure, and it is mine and my friends' sworn duty to keep it safe."

"You act like you know where it is." It was just a statement, but the way he phrased his comment was like he knew, and he nodded. "You can't know where it is?" Thinking, "It has been missing since...." I was trying to remember the year from my research.

"The year 1290." It was a quiet comment, but accurate. "What have you learned about the treasure, Victoria?"

Chapter 5

Highlands of Scotland

Grayson

Victoria was tenacious, and that stubbornness is getting her into a lot of trouble, she just didn't know how much. I asked her again when she just stared at me. "What have you learned about the treasure, Victoria?"

She straightened her shoulders, and spoke, "I am in my graduate studies at Stamford. Archeology." She started, "My professor got me interested in the treasure." She was looking at the flames as she talked. "I have been researching it for over a year now, for my thesis. When I learned about the book, I told you about, I told my professor and booked my trip." She looked back over to me, "How do you know so much about it?"

I decided to be direct and honest, "My grandfather was one of the knights that hid the treasure for Guillaume de Beaujeu. As I said it is my friends and I sworn duty to keep it safe."

Her brows came together as she was trying to do the math, "That can't be right, it was lost in 1290. Your grandfather would not have even been born, much less old enough to hide it. Or he was as old as Methuselah." She smiled at the jest she made.

I smiled, "He was old by human standards, and he didn't find his mate until he was a little over 400 years old just a little older than I am." I watched her facial expressions, as she tried to work it all out in her head. "I am a Lycan, Victoria."

Her eyes widened in shock and then disbelief. She whispered, "Fear -madadh-allaidh"

Impressed, Gaelic is not easy, but she pronounced the word correctly. "Not exactly wolf, Victoria. Lycans are different." I tried to explain.

Her fear was obvious, but she stayed where she was. "Lycans are a myth, made up." She said but her voice shook.

"Victoria, I am a Lycan, and you are my mate. I will protect you with my life." I didn't move, she was frightened, I could see it in her eyes as well as smell her fear. "And you trust me, I know you do."

She was looking down and shaking her head, but that statement brought her face back to mine. "I trust you?" The fear was still in her eyes as she whispered the question.

My voice was calm, "Victoria, you do trust me. Think about it, something deep down inside of you is telling you…"

Her eyes had not left my face, "Telling me what?" It was a harsh whisper.

I decided to try a different approach to get her to understand I extended my hand. "Victoria, come here, please. I will never harm you; I promise." My eyes didn't leave her face, and I was a little surprised when she did move toward me. She laid her hand on mine, I placed it on my chest close to my heart. "You said earlier that my chest moved, it was my beast." My t-shirt was thin, and we both could feel the warmth of her hand laying close to my heart. My beast nudged her hand, and she looked up.

"You are doing that on purpose." But when she looked into my eyes they had changed and glowed red. "Your eyes." She whispered.

"Yes, my eyes." I agreed. "I know Lycans have become a myth to most humans, and it is better for our kind that it is kept that way. But Victoria, we do exist." Smiling she since had not moved her hand from my chest. "And we are not the monsters you see in the movies."

Ever so slowly she removed her hand and sat back down where she had been before. "I am tired."

The rabbit had not been touched, but since she was trying to sort out what I had told her, I just nodded and got up, "Here I made you a soft spot to sleep. Keep the kilt you will need it." I showed her where I had gathered some moss for a makeshift mattress for her to lay. Once she was settled, I walked back over, resuming my place against the boulder again, closing my eyes. I knew she was going to run.

The second she stirred, my eyes opened, and I watched as she ran into the dense woods, I got up and walked in the direction she went, I could hear every twig that snapped under her feet, as well as see her. Sooner or later, she would either get stopped by one of the sentries or hurt in the dark.

I wasn't far behind her, when she ran straight into a sentry, she screamed in fear as he grabbed her arm. He was not in his full Lycan form, but he touched what is mine. Growling, I pulled her away from his grasp. *"MINE"* I roared. I was older and stronger, and he backed away.

"I am sorry, my prince." He bowed his head.

"My brother is 'My Prince' not me." I barked at him. I had grown at least three inches, and my fangs had elongated, as well as my claws.

"What is he?" She was terrified at the site of what looked like a half-man half-beast speaking.

"Go, now. She won't wander off again." The sentry backed away into the trees out of her sight, but I knew he was there watching us.

She looked up at me, "What are you?" she gasped at the site of my fangs and height. I caught her before she hit the ground when she fainted.

"I am a Lycan, Victoria, and you are mine," I whispered as I carried her back to the cave laying her down gently and covering her back up. The thought of chasing her when we first mate, thrilled me, but I didn't want to be chasing her all night long, so I stretched out beside her. Closing my eyes, I was content for the moment to lay beside her, then she snuggled against me, "Your body recognizes mine, even if you don't understand yet, Victoria." I whispered pulling her closer wrapping my arm around her and then kissing the top of her head.

Just as the first lights of the morning were streaming from the east my eyes opened, and I looked down. Victoria was still asleep with her hand on my heart. I hated the fact that I had to wake her, but Noah would be waiting, and we had to get back home. Kissing the top of her head, "Victoria, we need to leave soon." I whispered in her ear giving her a little shake.

She sat up with a start. "How?" She frowned at me seeing the intimate position she was in sleeping beside me. Shaking her head, "I had the strangest dream." She uttered still sleepy.

I had to get her to understand the truth, "It wasn't a dream, Victoria. You ran away and right into one of the sentries."

She turned her head and looked over to the woods, "He..." She turned back to me, "Your voice, and eyes and nails. You weren't lying." She mused with a hint of amazement.

"No, Victoria lying is something I don't do." I crooned and stood and moved over to make sure the fire was completely out, then holding out my hand, "I need to put the kilt away."

"It's true. You are a Lycan, and they are real." She muttered; I could see she was working it out in her head. I still had my hand held out, Victoria looked down at the kilt, "Oh, yes. Thank you." She stood tenderly folding the kilt before handing it back to me. "It is so soft, and it smells like you." She whispered the last part, but I heard every word.

It's yours then. My gift to you," I smiled, then placed the folded kilt in my pack. Taking out a pair of pants, I looked at her, "Stay here, I will be right back, I need to change." I walked to where I knew she could not see me, and dropped my kilt, slipping on my pants. Once I had claimed her, I would not care if she saw me naked or not, but she was still getting used to the idea of me, and I was trying to give her time. Coming back to the cave I put my saddlebags on my bike and said, "Now, Noah is waiting." I lifted her onto the bike, getting on in front of her, and instinctively she wrapped her hands around me. "We will stop for some breakfast once we meet up with Noah." Then I kicked started my bike.

I took a shorter route to get to where Noah and I were meeting up. Passing by the Wick River she pointed out the rapids flowing. "It's beautiful." Exclaiming at the site of the water flowing.

Looking at where she pointed, I agreed, "It is, though it looks like a nice place to swim, that current is also unpredictable and deadly." I called out over the noise of my motorcycle. Thankfully no one was up and about at this hour, so I could go as fast as I wanted. Victoria didn't notice, again I was thankful.

I knew she still must be tired; I patted her hand on my chest, "Close your eyes and lay your head on my back. It is still early yet, go back to sleep. I will not let you fall off." I felt her head lay on my back, and as soon as I felt her relax into sleep, I reached back and brought her around to cradle in my arms. She never woke up, just snuggled closer.

Once we were back in Wick, I pulled around to the back of the Old Pulteney Distillery. Noah was waiting, seeing that Victoria was asleep in my arms, he whispered. "There was a tracking device in her phone."

Victoria stirred, then frowned up at me holding her like a baby. "A what?" she asked looking over to Noah, "I am sorry, Noah, good morning." She yawned and stretched.

Noah had his legs braced apart, looking over to me, I nodded, "A tracking device. That is how they knew where to find you."

"How did you lose them?" I asked but I could already see Noah grinning.

"I caught a rabbit and tied the tracker around his neck then chased him off." Laughing, "They probably chased after that rabbit for a good hour, before it occurred to them, they had been duped." He was serious now, "Then, I circled back watching the castle for another two hours before heading here. They came back and looked around but didn't know to look up." Noah walked up to Victoria and handed her back her backpack.

"When does the ferry leave?" I asked him, looking around, it was still early, but the human workers would be arriving soon, though it was old, this is still an active distillery.

Noah looked at his watch, "In about thirty minutes. He said, "I already have all of our tickets."

"How did you get a ticket for me?" Then it dawned on her he had her backpack, "You used my passport." She wiggled to get loose, and I lifted her down, "I need to get back to my research." She held out her hand to me, "Thank you for the adventure."

I motioned to Noah to give us a moment alone. "Victoria, I cannot let you go on your own."

She folded her arms across her chest. I could not help but notice her ample breasts., "Why because I am your MATE?" There was sarcasm in her voice, she still had not accepted the truth.

I grinned mimicking her by folding my arms as well, "That and because you are still in danger, whatever you may think." Whistling Noah returned and I tossed him back her bag. I knew that research was too important for her not to follow. Looking at her, "Are you coming with us or not?" The woman had a fire inside of her, her eyes flared with anger as she glared at me and nodded.

I just grinned and held out my hand as she climbed on my bike behind me. Angry she whispered, "You are not always going to get your way with me, Mr. Lycan."

She didn't know I heard every word; I just patted her hands on my chest and teased, "Sure I will." Then I kickstarted my bike and followed Noah.

I heard her gasp, "What big ears you have!" She was still angry, as she recited a line from a children's story.

Watching the growing traffic as we traveled to the ferry, "Something like that." A car passed us a little too close, and I reached back holding Victoria making sure she didn't fall as I swerved. "Idiot," I called out.

"My god that was..." Her voice was filled with shock, "Grayson that was my professor."

Speeding up, I was beside Noah, "We have company!" I called over and pointed to the car that passed me.

He nodded and sped up; I was right behind him. Once we were on the ferry, Noah stayed with the bikes, I took Victoria's bag and her hand. Walking up to the top deck I passed the rows of bench seats until we reached the back of the ferry. It was still early, and the ferry was not full of people, but I wanted to put some distance between any innocents and trouble. Sitting down the railing behind us was the only thing that stopped us from falling into the freezing water below. I waited and watched as her professor and two others approached.

"Victoria, I want that clue!" The sneer came from a man that looked like Don Knotts. Then he and the other two moved their jackets to the side showing that they each were armed.

I just shook my head, "She doesn't have it." My voice was calm and controlled but deeper. Professor didn't know that, but Victoria did. "And those guns are useless against me." Standing I grew in front of them my fangs came out as I spoke as I put myself between them and Victoria.

The only smart one of the three whispered "Madadhallaidh." Turning running straight into Noah standing behind them. Noah just reached into his jacket and took the gun, tossing it over the side into the water, before stepping aside and letting the man pass. The second man looked back to Noah and watched as he too grew and snarled and showed his fangs to him.

Shaking his head, he removed his gun, and tossed it over the side, "You can't pay me enough for this." Running past Noah, "I am going to be in therapy for years."

Professor losing his back up pointed his gun directly at my chest, I saw him glance at her backpack, shaking my head at Noah telling him not to intervene. "Not a wolf a Lycan." He snarled, "Well, I guess I will just have to go get some silver bullets for the next time we meet." He walked backward as he spoke, "Victoria, I will get what I want!" He called out before he disappeared down the stairs.

I kept Victoria where she was until we docked at Kirkwall, Scotland, we moved our bikes out of the way and waited until all the passengers that included Professor were off the ferry before leaving. "Plane's waiting on the tarmac," Noah announced.

"Did you tell them about our visitor?" Asking as I put a shocked Victoria on my bike, handing Noah her backpack. She had not said anything since her professor pointed a gun at me.

"Aye, they will be on the lookout." He got on his bike, and we headed toward a private Lycan-owned landing stripe of Kirkwall airport. The plane was already on the runway, with the tail lowered. Two Lycan guards opened the gate as we passed and drove directly up into the plane. I lifted Victoria down, "You take care of her, I will secure the bikes." Noah's voice was laced with concern for Victoria.

Victoria blinked, "Where are we going?"

She was coming out of her shock, "Home." I answered and led her up to the cabin to get settled. "But first we are going to stop off in Edinburgh to pick up a book." As I sat across from her, "Tell me where the journal is located in the library, please."

Chapter 6

Victoria

Grayson said we were going to get a book, looking up at him, "You mean the old journal I got the information from?"

His eyes never left my face, "Yes, we must keep the treasure safe from humans. Can you tell me where it is located in the library? I would hate to have to tear the place apart looking for it." He explained with a grin.

The back of the plane rose before we took off down the runway. Noah came up and sat a few rows away from us. Leaning back, he closed his eyes, looking relaxed. But I had a feeling he was not asleep or relaxed. He was just giving me time alone with Grayson, for which I was grateful. "It is in the heritage collections. On the sixth floor." I answered him. "It's the diary of William Sinclair the Second Earl." I offered and even showed him a picture that I had taken.

Grayson nodded and thanked me. I was still thinking about the events that happened on the ferry, I looked up at Grayson, "He pointed a gun at you." My voice trembled, "You didn't seem afraid, he could have killed you."

"Would that have upset you if he shot me, Victoria?" His voice was soft, and his eyes I just noticed are the same shade of green as mine. His hair was a strawberry blonde, and short on top, trimmed on the sides with Gaelic symbols. He wore an earring in his left ear, and his beard fell to the top of his chest. Something inside of me was drawn to him, and he was right. I did trust him with my life.

"Of course, I would be upset." I realized I had not answered him. He was watching me and smiling. "Why are you smiling?" I asked a little irritated at his grin.

He leaned back still grinning at me and mused, "I was just watching you working it all out in your head." He uttered.

I just shook my head, still a little irritated muttered, "I seem to amuse you a lot."

Grayson leaned forward reaching across the table between us for my hand, "I am not laughing at you, Victoria. I am happy I found you after all these years." His voice was soft and gentle.

I placed my hand in his large one, "How many years?" I inquired.

"It is a Lycan's nature to find their fated mate nearly from birth." He explained. "And, I have been searching for you for over four hundred years."

My eyes never left his face, "I am not sure I understand all of this." I said softly more to myself than to him.

"I know, but we will get to know each other." He turned serious, "Victoria, I will never hurt you and I will protect you with my life if need be. But know, I cannot and will never give you up." He smiled and tapped the side of his nose, "I have your scent." Then moving his hand to his chest, "We have your scent." I believed everything he said.

We had been in the air for just about an hour, when a voice came over the speaker, "We are about to land in Edinburgh, sirs." Noah and Grayson both stood.

"Victoria, you stay on the plane, the guards will protect you," Grayson ordered.

I think it was pure instinct that made me reach out for Grayson's hand, "Please be careful." Then looking over to Noah, "Both of you."

Grayson leaned down and kissed the top of my head, "We will, Mo Chara."

I heard Noah chuckling, "She is beginning to sound like Samantha." As they walked down the stairs to the cargo area of the plane.

When the plane stopped, I heard the back lower and I watched out the window as Grayson and Noah, on their bikes weaved around the plane and headed toward Edinburgh. I paced around, looking for my backpack, and paced some more. Moving towards the stairs that lead down to the cargo area, "I am sorry Miss, I can't let you go down there." A deep voice said, I turned to see a large man standing behind me. "It is too dangerous down there for you, and I have my orders to keep you safe." He didn't touch me, and I knew he would never do so. I nodded; I would not get him into trouble by disobeying his orders.

"Yes, thank you. I was looking for my backpack." I answered. Then I moved back to where I was sitting. Moments later, the guard returned and laid my backpack on the table.

"Here you go, Miss." He stated and returned to where he had been standing before.

I opened my backpack, "Thank you," I said looking over my shoulder at where the guard stood. Reaching into my back-pack, I first pulled out my research notebooks and then my laptop. Remembering what Noah said about a tracer on my phone, I decided not to turn it on, and just read through my handwritten notes. I became engrossed and did not realize how much time had passed.

My head lifted, when I heard the tail of the plane lower back down, a few moments later, Grayson and Noah rode back on the plane. The guard had his finger to his ear and then looked over at me, "Miss, I need you please buckle your seat belt, we need to leave now!" There was an urgency in the guard's voice I didn't understand, but I did as he requested.

Grayson came up the stairs holding onto his left shoul-der, there was blood seeping between his fingers. "Grayson!" I shouted in concern and unbuckling my seatbelt I ran to him.

Running back to my backpack I grabbed a clean t-shirt. Grayson had sat down in a seat, as the plane took off. "I will be fine." He persisted. But he didn't look fine, I moved his hand away and tore open his shirt at the bullet hole. He just watched as I pressed my t-shirt to the wound.

Noah had come up the stairs, I snapped at him, "What happened?" He backed up at the tone of my voice.

"Your professor friend was there and another we were afraid was hunting the treasure. Just as we were coming out, and..." He stopped speaking and watched me hold the pressure on the wound. "The bullet is stuck in his bone, and he can't expel it." Noah finally said.

I wasn't sure I understood what he was saying, "We need to get him to a hospital!" I demanded.

Grayson reached up and stroked my face with his right hand, "Humans can't help me." He said, then looked up at Noah, "Tell them to head to Fergus' holding outside of Dunalstair, and call ahead tell them what we need, and then call Lucas." Noah nodded and headed to the cockpit to give the orders.

Chapter 7

Grayson

Noah and I weaved our way through Edinburgh traffic from the airport. Getting to the University was easy. Parking in the back of the library building, we took the back stairs to the sixth floor. Noah had to use his tools to unlock the door, once open we quietly slipped through. The librarians on duty never noticed us, and we were thankful. We didn't want any innocents in harm's way if there was trouble.

Victoria told me which row and shelf the journal was located on, and I found it easily. I slipped the leather-bound journal into the back of my pants and pulled my shirt over it. We were coming out of the aisle when we saw her professor at the librarian's desk. He looked up and our eyes met across the space of the large room. He glared at me and immediately turned to leave.

Turning my head, I whispered to Noah behind me, "The professor is here." We turned and walked around in the opposite direction back to the door we came in. We took the stairs two at a time, hoping to leave before he found us. Coming out of the back door we reached our bikes just a car sped to a screeching halt a few feet away from us.

The professor opened the door as he swung a gun around, he screamed, "The treasure is mine." Firing a shot, it was wide and hit the building to our left.

Both Noah and I got on our bikes, kickstarting them, and started to leave just as the second bullet rang out. I felt the bullet as it landed in my clavicle, and I swerved nearly losing control. But I managed to stay upright, but as hard I tried the bullet would not expel. I knew I was vulnerable and could cost us this mission. Calling over to Noah, "I can't get the bullet out! Take the book and go!"

Noah reached over and took the book from the back of my pants. I slowed to try again to get the bullet to come loose and expel but it was no good. But I had managed to stay on my Harley. Coming around to the front of the library, I saw him, Tavish. He had changed his appearance again, but it was him for sure.

He saw me too, there was a smirk on his face as he saluted me. Then pointing his finger at me as if pointing a gun, he laughed. And turned down a street away from me. He must have been there and seen everything that happened. I was in no shape to go after him, and we needed to get the journal and clue back home.

Noah was ahead of me but was still close enough that he could turn around and come back. As I drove I kept my eyes on his back and tried to stay upright on my bike as we headed toward the airport. I could hear the professor's car not far behind me. Even with my blood seeping down my arm, causing the handle to become slick and sticky, I swerved around cars keeping my back out of line for another direct shot. I also prayed he would not try to shoot at us again with all these humans strolling up and down the streets.

The airport was not far now, and I saw Noah pull his cell out and call to have the gate opened and the tail lowered. I rode up the ramp into the cargo area of the plane and stopped. Noah was right there beside me, assuring him. "I will be okay, get the bikes secure and hide the book and clue. We need to leave. The professor was close behind us."

Noah nodded, "Aye."

Lifting my right hand, I put some pressure on the wound but my blood was still flowing and seeped out between my fingers. I got up the stairs to the passenger area of the plane and sat in the nearest seat.

Victoria turned as I sat, shouting my name she didn't hesitate to unbuckle her seatbelt to run to me. Only once did she leave my side, and that was to get a shirt from her backpack. Tears were falling from her eyes as she pushed my hand away and tore open my shirt to examine the wound. Then she placed her shirt on my shoulder and pushed with all her might.

When Noah came up, she snapped at him demanding to know what happened. Noah was shocked at her outburst and tried to explain the events but noticed that she was more concerned that I would not stop bleeding. So, he explained that I could not expel the bullet, and she insisted that I be taken to a human hospital.

I reached up and stroked her cheek to wipe away the tears I didn't even think she knew she had shed when I told her that humans could not help me.

Then I looked up to Noah and gave him orders to take us back to Fergus' estate and call Lucas and explain what happened. Noah nodded then turned and did as I ordered.

We landed about an hour later, Victoria was still pressing her shirt to my shoulder when two of Fergus' men came in. We both looked up as they nodded, "They need to help me off the plane, Mo chara." I whispered. Victoria nodded and stepped back as they helped me stand and out of the plane.

I was helped into a waiting SUV and taken to Fergus' house. Once they got me inside a back room, that was equipped with medical supplies, I was laid out on a table. A Lycan came in wearing scrubs and resembling a human doctor. He removed Victoria's shirt and examined the wound. "Looks like you had some trouble." He hummed as he probed at my shoulder.

"Yeah," I answered. Noah walked in and was standing guard by the door. "Where's Victoria?" I asked through clenched teeth.

Noah responded, "She is fine, Fergus is bringing her back and taking care of her."

This Lycan so-called doctor was taking his time, "Just get the fuckin' thing out of my bone." I barked then saw Noah smile and lower his head to hide it.

What seemed like hours was only about forty-five minutes, until he was able to get the bullet free. I was ready to tear his head off by the time he pulled the bullet out with a clamp. "There she is." He hummed. No stitches were needed as soon as the bullet was out, and the wound closed on its own. He wrapped my arm and shoulder then had Fergus' men take me upstairs and laid me out on a bed. Victoria's scent was all around the room, so I knew this was the room, Fergus had put Victoria in. Comforted by just having her scent near me I closed my eyes until she returned.

Chapter 8

Victoria

Two men came in and left with Grayson. I turned from where I was standing to gather my research. Looking down at my hands, they were covered with Grayson's blood. It was too much. I sat down with my hands folded on the table, shaking with fear. I had an overwhelming hatred toward my professor. He shot another person for that stupid treasure; he probably wouldn't have second thoughts about killing me to get to it.

My mind was still swirling around in thoughts when I felt a hand on my shoulder, looking up there was an older man, standing there. "I am Fergus Donnachaidh, Samantha's father. You are on my land now, and no one can hurt you. If you please come with me, I will get you settled while my men are taking care of Grayson."

I just nodded and stood. I gathered up my notebooks and laptop putting them back in my backpack then followed the man out to a waiting SUV. He opened the door for me, and I got in. I was still in shock, and had not said anything to him, realizing my rudeness, "Thank you for taking us in, and helping Grayson." I murmured.

His smile was genuine as he nodded, "He is my cousin and a dear friend of my daughter and her mate. I would not refuse to help him." Looking at the worried look on my face, "Grayson will be fine as soon as they get the bullet out of his bone, you will see." Then he patted my knee just as my father does, I could not help but smile.

We arrived at a very old stone manor, he led me up the stairs to a bedroom, "You can clean up and rest in here." Turning to leave, "On second thought, you get cleaned up, and I will have some food prepared for you when you come down."

Stepping further into the room, I looked around at the lush furniture and fabrics on the bed. Talking to myself, *'I don't think I am in Kansas anymore.'* I found the bathroom and took a quick shower then dressed. I felt out of place here, these people were made of money, and all I had to wear was another pair of jeans and a t-shirt. But there was nothing I could do, at least my clothes were clean. So, I retraced the path we took to the room, and heading down the stone staircase, I looked at the paintings on the walls, they had to be hundreds of years old and worth a fortune. Samantha's father waiting for me, and I smiled. "We are slowly getting everything back in its proper place." I didn't know what he meant, but I continued down, as I reached the bottom, he took my hand and folded it in the crook of his arm leading me into a dining room.

As he seated me at the table, "How is Grayson doing?" I uttered.

"They have got the bullet out of the bone and are dressing his wound now." He looked at me, "I know you are human, and all of this is new and confusing to you." Again, he patted my hand, "Grayson can start his healing process now, and I will take you to him as soon as you eat."

What I assumed were servants carried trays with large amounts of food to the table. The only time I had seen this amount of food was when my father had splurged, and we took a trip to Las Vegas. This reminded me of one of the buffets there. Noah came in shortly and sat down nodding to our host. "I spoke to Lucas, as soon as Grayson is able, we need to be on our way. He sends his thanks for your assistance. And Samantha added..." He coughed "...her love." I swore that the giant of a man blushed.

When I finished, I looked at Noah, "May I see Grayson now?" I didn't want to interrupt his meal, he just nodded and stood. I followed him back up to the room where I changed and there on the bed Grayson was laying. His shoulder had a bandage on it, and he looked to be sleeping. "Thank you," I whispered as Noah quietly retreated and closed the door.

I pulled up a chair and sat beside Grayson. "I am fine, Victoria." He opened his eyes, patting the bed on the other side of him, "Come lay down with me." Not thinking I moved to the other side of the bed and laid down propping my head up on my hand. He looked over at me, "Are you going to watch me all night?" He smiled at the thought.

The blanket was pulled down to his waist and his chest was bare. A sprinkling of hair covered his chest following down the rippled abs that disappeared under the covers. His chest has a Gaelic tattoo. "You could have been killed." Whispering. I was not sure where it came from, but a tear trailed down my cheek.

Grayson reached up and whipped the tear away, then wrapped his right arm around me, pulled me down, and kissed me. It was not a chaste kiss by any means, hungrily he probed my mouth with his tongue demanding entrance. I wanted this, and I knew in my soul, I wanted him. At that moment I gave in to those feelings and opened my mouth. My hand was on his chest, and I felt the movement of what he called his beast under it. Pulling away, I looked into his eyes, they had turned red, but I was not afraid. Leaning back down I kissed him, our tongues dueled in each other's mouths, and soon it was becoming apparent that kissing was not going to be enough. I moaned with pleasure as he rolled over covering me with his body, "Your shoulder!" I pushed him back some.

"Hush... I am fine." His voice deepened, and his fangs were growing. "Are you afraid of me, Victoria?" He nuzzled his nose in the curve of my neck. I shook my head no, "Good." His breath was heavy as he came back up to my mouth, "You have too many clothes on." He sighed, "But this is not the time or place for me to claim you. When we get home, and on the next full moon, I will make you mine." Then he leaned down and captured my mouth for another ravenous kiss.

Pulling away from me, a growl of disappointment came from deep within him as he rolled back bringing me with him. "Are you okay?" I asked concerned about his shoulder.

His breathing was heavy, "No." Taking my hand he brought it his massive hard-on "I want you." His voice was gruff. "And I can smell your desire for me, Victoria."

A breathless "Oh." Came from me feeling his hard-on under the blanket.

He turned his head to me, smiling. "It is all for you, mo chara!" Then he pulled my hand away from his cock and laid it on his chest. "Soon, I promise. When we get home." Then he put my head on his shoulder, "We need to rest before we leave." I closed my eyes, smiling as I drifted off to sleep.

Chapter 9

Grayson

Another morning was here, and again Victoria was curled up on my side. I sighed with pleasure as I thought. *'This was how we will be every morning for the rest of our lives. But Victoria will have a lot fewer clothes on.'* Slowly I moved her away and sat up. Rolling my wounded arm, I pulled the bandage off and was reaching for my pants. "How do you feel?" It was Victoria's sleepy voice.

I turned and looked at her, rolling my arm again, "Healed." I insisted then sighed, "Victoria, I need to put my pants on, and I am not wearing anything under this blanket." I explained as I stood up letting her get a good look at my naked backside.

"Oh!" she yelped giggling as she hid her face in the pillows. After I got my pants up, I turned around and gave her a little slap on her nice round ass.

"You need to get used to me, and we need to get home." I turned back to get a shirt from my bag that was brought up. Victoria jumped off the bed, came around she stood in front of me.

She was focused on the wound, running her finger over the small and hardly noticeable mark on my shoulder. Looking up at me, "It looks like it is completely healed."

I held her face up to mine, "Lycans can self-heal. Because the bullet was lodged in my bone, I could not expel it, they had to cut it out. But once it was out, I could heal on my own." Victoria's eyes never left my face. But she had rested one of her hands on my chest. My beast nudged it, and she smiled. I leaned down and gave her a quick light kiss on the lips. "Can you be ready to leave in an hour?"

She pulled away, "Yes, probably faster." She said and patted my chest before grabbing her backpack, she dashed into the bathroom. Victoria was true to her word of being faster coming down about thirty minutes later. Fergus and his men drove us out to the awaiting plane. Victoria got out of the car and looked at Fergus' hand ignoring it she stretched up kissing him on his cheek and thanking him for his hospitality and help.

He patted her cheek, "You are going to give him a run for his money, I can see it." He grinned. I reached out shaking his hand and thanked him as well. Victoria had moved to my side and watched the exchange.

"I expect an invitation to the formal ceremony." Then he added as he glanced back to Victoria, "I had some food packed up and put on the plane for all of you." Fergus explained then addressing her, "Victoria, I have a gift for Samantha, would you mind giving it to her for me." He turned as one of his men handed him a wrapped package that he then handed to her.

"Of course, sir." She smiled, "I have heard wonderful things about her, and cannot wait to meet her." Patting the package, she carried it with her up the stairs into the plane. We were in the air moments later.

"What have you heard about Samantha?" I wondered out loud. Victoria was looking at her research notebooks.

She looked up, "Noah keeps saying I sound more and more like her. So, she must be a wonderful person of course." After making that statement she grinned at me, glancing over her shoulder to Noah, and back to me she winked. All I could do is laugh; this mate of mine was going to give me a run for my money as Fergus said. I leaned back and closed my eyes.

"I found it!" Victoria exclaimed some hours later.

I opened my eyes, "Found what?" Looking at the notebook she had open in front of her.

"The reason, Professor Maxwell wants the treasure so bad." She was pointing to her notes. "I had done a genealogy search on him when I first started. He thinks he is a descendant of Guillaume de Beaujeu. I remember him telling me that he was his descendant and that the treasure belonged to him. But he isn't. I wrote it all down here in my notes."

"You have all this written out when you have your laptop?" I started to reach for her laptop.

She stopped my hand. "It is all on there, but I remembered that Noah said that my phone had a tracer on it, so I thought I need to get my laptop to a tech, to make sure there are no viruses on there that could trace my location."

"Levi can take a look at it when we get home," I told her; she tilted her head to the side in confusion. "He is another friend of ours and a computer genius." I looked at her, "Why did you want to find it, Victoria?"

She just shrugged her shoulders, "Student loans." Her mouth quirked up into a small smile, "I'm in debt up to my eyeballs and I need to pay them off and help my father. I have been in school for a long time. But there are so many different theories of what the treasure is, some say it is a vast fortune, and I have read that it could be the chalice from the Last Supper. Still worth a great deal." She shrugged her shoulders. "Even though I thought he had been using his students to search for the treasure for him. I now know that he is willing to kill for it." Closing her notebook, "When I get home, I will have to look for a new topic for my thesis, and a job," she sounded defeated.

When she said she intended to go home, my stomach lurched. She still didn't understand the significance of being mated to a Lycan. I was not worried; we would work it all out. But she looked tired, her eyes were red from reading for hours. "What you need to do right now is get some rest. You have been looking at your notes for hours." I said as I stood, taking her hand and moving down a table that turned into a bed, getting a pillow, then my kilt from my bag. "Get some sleep." She curled up, and I sat beside her to make sure she didn't fall if we hit any turbulence. Leaning back, I closed my eyes again. As she fell asleep her hand came to rest on my leg, I placed it on top of hers and held it there.

It was a long flight from Scotland to the United States, Victoria slept for a good while before I woke her up. Leaning down I growled low in her ear, "Mo Chara, you need to wake up." Her hand reached out and stroked my beard, then she sat up and stretched. I was pleased with how she became accustomed to and relaxed around me. She was going to be a wonderful mate, and I presumed she would not take to being bossed around.

"You are smiling at me again." She was frowning at me, then she crossed her arms over her chest. "Why?"

I just shook my head and kissed her nose. "Because I want to smile at you, Mo Chara." She rolled her eyes and shook her head, "Are you hungry?" I asked ignoring her exasperation.

That got her attention, "Oh yes. Are you?" She answered. Looking around, "Where are Noah and the others? They must be hungry too."

I liked the way she thought of the others, "They are down in the cargo area." Replying.

She frowned at me, "It must be freezing down there! Grayson, please ask them to come up, while I fix the food for everyone." It was not exactly an order, but I grunted just to see her expression.

The one she gave me was priceless a mix of irritation and frustration. I just grinned then went to the stairs letting out a loud piercing whistle down. I laughed when she jumped. "It's loud down there." Explaining. Noah came up, "Victoria is warming the food, tell the others to come up and eat." He glanced over to Victoria glaring at me and nodded. Disappearing back down the stairs.

I went over to the galley where she was now working on warming the food bracing my hands on both sides of her hips against the counter. Nuzzling her neck, I whispered, "I didn't mean to startle you." She tilted her head to one side sighing at the intimacy of my breath on her neck. I could not help but breathe in deep, "You smell so good."

"It's the food." She quipped back.

"No, it is the scent of your desire for me," I whispered back. All I could think was I wished we were home, I wanted nothing more than to lay her down and spread her legs so I could feast on her.

She turned around and looked over my shoulder, "You can smell that I am....?" Just then Noah and the others started to come back up and sat down. Her cheeks turned bright red with embarrassment. "Can they smell it too?"

"You are cute when you are blushing all red." I was grinning, "Yes, but they would not ever dare mention it."

She was shocked at my statement, "I am going to die of em- barrassment if I walk in there." I could tell she was genuinely distressed.

Victoria had lowered her head, "Victoria, look at me." I was still whispering though I knew the others could hear us. "They would never dare to do or say anything to harm or embarrass you in any way. You are my mate, they respect that." She had tears in her eyes, "Each of them would lay down their lives to protect you if needed. Just as we all would do for Samantha and little Kelvin."

She sniffed back the tears and wiped her eyes. Nodding she lifted her head high and started to lay out the plates for each of the men. When none of them started to eat, she looked at me confused. "As their hostess, they are waiting on you to sit down to eat as well," I explained. Understanding, she sat beside me to eat.

After they each finished, each man stood and bowed to her and thanked her for the meal. Cleaning up as they went. Again, she was confused by their actions. "They are just being polite. Lycans are at times more civilized than humans." Standing I took her plate, and thanked her, going into the galley to clean up for her. But she came in to help anyways.

Once we sat back down, "Tell me about your home, please." She asked.

"It is your home too, I built it with you in mind." But when she didn't respond, I continued, "We have land outside of the city, quite a bit of land by human standards surrounded by rolling hills with dense woods. And a very old mine. Each of us built homes with our mates in mind. They are built in a circle, so we each can see the front of the other houses, in case of trouble." I continued to describe our compound to her, and she sat and listened without interrupting me, she was smiling as I talked.

Soon the pilot announced that we were going to land in about thirty minutes. "You will get to see everything very soon." She gathered up her laptop and notebooks putting them into her backpack. I took it from her and looked down in, "You don't have a lot of clothes."

She laughed, "I have more clothes than you see there. They are all just in my apartment outside of campus." She smiled as she explained.

"I will send someone to retrieve them and anything else you want from your apartment." My voice was stern, letting her know I was not going to argue about this.

Shocked, "You won't let me get my things?" Her eyes flashed with anger, as she grumbled. "I am not used to being ordered around Grayson."

Catching her around the waist, "Until I can make sure you are no longer in danger from your professor, I will be keeping you close to me. And you are my mate, I will protect you always." She was not happy and tried to push my arm away so she could get off the plane. "Victoria!" I barked, "I will not let you get hurt!"

She turned in my arms, tears streaming down her face. "You already have been hurt, Grayson!" I don't think she realized that she was yelling at me. I knew it was out of fear for my safety.

Lucas came up behind her, "Is everything okay?" His voice was quiet, but she jumped at the sound anyways.

She brushed her tears away before turning to face Lucas, "Yes! But your friend is an incorrigible beast!" She snapped.

Lucas was standing with his legs braced apart his arms crossed over his chest and grinning like a fool, "I have noticed that from time to time about him. I am Lucas Cain." He offered.

Victoria held out her hand, "I am Victoria Campbell, you may call me Vickie. Supposedly I am that one's mate." She tilted her head towards me then thinking for a moment, "Lucas? You are Samantha's husband?"

Lucas could not help but smile at her fury at me. "She is my mate, yes." He replied.

Victoria just rolled her eyes. "It amounts to the same thing in my mind. But I have a gift for her from her father."

She reached for her backpack, "I will get that for you." I stated.

Glaring back at me, "I don't think so." She snapped, turning back to Lucas, "If you could please take me to her." Her voice was sweet when she addressed Lucas.

Lucas looked over her head speaking to her even though he was looking at me, "Victoria, I think Grayson should bring you to back." He was still grinning at me like a lunatic, totally amused that this little human was in no way intimidated by my size or strength. He turned and called over his shoulder as he descended the stairs, "I will be happy to introduce you to Samantha as soon as you arrive." His laughter filled the stairway as he left the plane.

She took two steps towards the stairs; I caught her around the waist again and sat down bringing her with me onto my lap. "What was that all about? Clothes or me being shot?" I demanded in a much quieter tone.

Her head was lowered. "Shot, I guess." She whispered. "You scared me to death."

I was nuzzling her neck again, "So you can understand how I would feel if you were to get hurt?" I asked.

She just nodded, "You still scared the shit out of me." She mumbled.

I chucked, "I think that is only the second time I heard you swear."

She took a deep calming breath, "My mother would wash my mouth out with soap if she heard me. It isn't ladylike. You probably won't hear me do it often." Tapping the side of her head, "Drummed in there."

I kissed her behind her ear, and she sighed, "I will have to teach you some dirty words for when we mate." She squirmed and giggled, holding her hips still, I decided to give her a little taste of what I meant, "Victoria, I am going to fuck you all night when we mate under the next full moon. I am going to lick up all those sweet juices I can smell dripping from your cunt. And you are going to moan and scream with pleasure as I thrust my cock in you." Her heart was racing, I could see it, and her arousal was the sweetest smell. I kissed her again then lifted her off my lap, "Now, we need to get going, or Samantha will send out a search party soon."

She stood up and looked up at me, her eyes were dilated from the images I just placed in her head, I was pretty much in the same shape as her, the full moon could not rise soon enough. But maybe I will just get a taste of her tonight. I took her backpack from her hand and led her out of the plane.

My bike had been parked just at the bottom of the stair-case. Before I lifted her on, I tossed her backpack to a waiting guard. "They will bring it back in one of the trucks. The air is warm, feel like a nighttime ride in the country?" I held out my hand to her.

She smiled and took my hand and I put her up on the back of my bike. Kickstarting it she wrapped her hands around my chest and stroked. My beast replied by nudging her hand. Yes, I thought, tonight I am going to get a taste of her sweet pussy and teach her some more dirty words.

Chapter 10

Victoria

I think Grayson took the long way back from the plane to where he lived, but I didn't mind. My imagination was running wild with the images of what he whispered in my ear. *"Victoria, I am going to fuck you all night under the next full moon. And you are going to moan and scream with pleasure as I thrust my cock in you."*

I remember what he felt like the other night, his cock was huge! I have spent my life with my nose in books, I didn't date, and I'm a virgin, I think I need to tell him. Sighing I was not sure how I was going to bring up that topic of conversation. *'Hey, Grayson...guess what I am a virgin, and your cock is going to rip me to shreds!'* Yeah, that is going to be a great way to start a conversation.

Sensing my nervousness, Grayson patted my hand, "Are you okay? You are as stiff as a board back there."

I took a deep breath and tried to relax, "Yes I am fine." I called out. *'Lair, Lair!'* I thought.

Since he pulled over, I assumed that he didn't believe me. Stopping the bike, he got off and then lifted me, "What's wrong?" He asked leaning on his bike, his legs stretched out and crossed at the ankles, as well as his arms crossed over his chest. "Victoria, please tell me what is going on in that head of yours."

Huffing, "Fine, what you described back in the plane." I snapped pacing back and forth.

He just nodded and grinned, "You got excited! I could..." he started to say.

"Please don't tell me again you could smell me." I held up my hand. "There is something I need to tell you." He uncrossed his ankles, took a hold of my hand pulling me between his legs.

Once I was there, he held on to my hips, "Tell me." It was a soft demand, but he was not letting me go back to my pacing.

"I'm a virgin!" I just blurted it out. "And you are huge!" I could not look at him I was so embarrassed by this conversation.

Grayson put his fingers under my chin and brought my face back up to look at him, "Victoria, are you afraid I am going to hurt you when we mate?" his voice was soft as he asked, but there was a smug grin on his face.

He had not moved his fingers, "Of course I am afraid." I whispered, then tried to look around, this was an awkward conversation at best, but I didn't want anyone else to hear us. "Grayson, I felt you. You are not going to fit." I tried to nod to get my point across.

Grayson moved his hand, "First there is no one near that can hear us. And second. Yes, when I first come into you, it will hurt. But, only for a moment or two, but I will only come into you when you are ready for me." He had one hand around my waist and the other he threaded his fingers around the back of my neck. "And Victoria, I am a virgin too." His eyes glowed.

"What? How! You know so much!" I exclaimed. "That can't be true. You are teasing me, and this is serious."

His hand was messaging the back of my neck, "I am telling you the truth." I had put my hands on his chest, and his beast moved. "Lycan's only mate for life. I have never been with another female, Lycan, or human in my life."

He wasn't lying to me I knew he was telling me the truth. "I just don't understand Lycans. Do you have a book I could read?" I was serious and he grinned at me.

"I am not sure there is one. But I will tell you anything you want to know." He pulled me closer to him and captured my mouth. I opened my mouth and let him kiss me hard, wrapping my hands around his neck. My tongue was just as active in his mouth as he was in mine, I moaned when he cupped my ass in his hands.

Moments passed when he pulled away, and turned his head, "The truck isn't far off."

I just stepped back, "Let me guess you can smell them." It was a jest.

Lifting me and putting on his bike, "No, I can hear them. Big ears remember." He swung his leg over his bike and started it back up. "But I think we need to finish this conversation later at home." He was grinning at the thought.

We turned onto an old road, and there was a guard that opened a gate for us. It was dark and I could not see much of what we were passing, but a few minutes later, we pulled up to what he had described to me on the plane, a circle of six houses. Stopping in front of a two-story stone house, the windows had twelve panes and the trim was painted brown and white, a porch stretched across the front. "It's gorgeous!" I was looking up, then back to Grayson. He was watching me, there was a sense of pride in his eyes.

Taking my hand, "Before I show you inside, I want to introduce you to Samantha, and I need to talk to Lucas. Okay?"

"Yes, of course." I looked around for the truck, "The gift is in my backpack." Just as I finished speaking and as Grayson had said, an SUV which must have been a minute behind us, pulled up. Grayson walked over and pulled my backpack out of the back, handing it to me. Reaching in I pulled out the gift, and a guard came up and took my bag for me. "Thank you." I nodded as he took it to the front of Grayson's home.

I followed Grayson to a modern house; it had a porch that looked like it wrapped all the way around. He knocked on the door, and Lucas opened it. Smiling, "I hope everything is better now?" As he gestured for us to enter.

I smiled back at him, "Yes, it is much better, thank you." I looked around Lucas, and behind him stood a lovely woman about my age. Her hair was so red, it was nearly orange and all curls. She was holding a baby on her hip; he was the spitting image of his father.

"Lucas. Your manners." She called out walking up behind him.

He just grinned, "Victoria, this is Samantha, my mate. And that is Kelvin our son, she is holding."

She walked up to me and lifted her son to his father. "Your turn." Taking the baby from his mother, "Victoria, come in the kitchen. I will make some tea, and we can get to know one another." Lucas just took the baby and turned to head to his office, nodding to Grayson to follow.

I did the same and just followed Samantha to the kitchen. "Your home is lovely." I was looking around that the modern kitchen.

She smiled, "I didn't have anything to do with that. Lucas built the house before we met." She started to hum as she put a tea kettle on the stove. "Come and sit down, I have heard you have had a trying couple of days. You must be tired and over-whelmed as well." She was moving around the kitchen placing cups and then a plate of cookies, on the table.

As I sat, I realized I had her father's gift in my hands. "Oh, I am sorry." I got up and walked to where she stood, "I forgot I had this in my hands. Your father asked me to give this to you. He was so sweet and helpful when Grayson was shot."

Her head snapped up. "Did you say SHOT?"

"Yes, I am sorry I thought you knew." I was trying to explain. She just excused herself and walked toward where Lucas and Grayson were. "Noah said he called and spoke to Lucas." I continued as I was chasing after her.

Once she arrived at the threshold of the office, "Shot!" She growled at both men. "You were shot?" She was glaring at Grayson then turned her face to Lucas, "And YOU didn't tell me!" Walking over to Lucas she snatched the baby out of his arms and turned and walked out of the room.

My mouth was open, she had yelled at them both. And neither moved to say or do anything about it, they just stared after her. Thinking about it, Grayson has never but the one time on the plane grumbled at me. Recognizing that I was star- ing, "I am sorry I thought she already knew." I turned quickly walking back into the kitchen.

Samantha was pacing back and forth, "I bet it was a retched human." Turning she looked over to me, "I am sorry, I was held by humans for ten years, and they killed my mother in front of me." Taking a deep breath, "I don't like to talk about it much, I know you are human, and I want us to be friends."

With a deep breath, "I'm pretty sure it was my professor that shot him." I sat back down at the table and just looked at my hands, "I should probably go home, I have caused too much trouble, and Grayson could have died because of me."

Samantha put the baby in a highchair, laying a cookie down on the tray in front of him. "Grayson will not let you go, Victoria." She sighed, "What do you know about Lycan's and our ways?"

I looked up at her, "Nothing." My voice was unhappy, "I didn't even really know you truly existed until I met Grayson." With a weak smile, "I asked him if there was a book I could read, but he said he didn't know of one."

Just then the tea kettle started to whistle, getting up she poured the water into the awaiting pot. "I don't think there is one either. But I do know of a human that is mated with another cousin of mine." Sitting back down she poured tea and both of our cups. "I will contact her and see if they can come for a visit then you can talk with her." After a moment of thought, she continued. "I would love to see Rose again too."

"Rose?" I asked as I sipped at my tea.

Samantha smiled, "Rose, was about three when Lucas found me. She too had been taken captive by the humans that held me. They were trying to sell her."

I could not believe what I was hearing, but the look in her eyes told me she was telling the truth, "You must hate me and all humans." I stood, "I never should have come here, I am sorry I am bringing up so many bad memories." Tears were streaming down my face. I started to walk towards the front door but realized that Grayson would see me. Then turned in the other direction to some French doors. "It was a pleasure meeting you. Please tell Grayson I said goodbye."

As soon as my feet hit the soft grass of the lawn, I ran. I didn't have any destination in mind I just ran. It was dark, but I didn't care. I was sure I would find a road sooner or later. And I was sure I heard Samantha call out to Lucas.

I was out of breath when I came to a clearing. Sitting down I leaned up against a tree, I lowered my head, I didn't know what to do. "Grayson was hurt all because of me. Samantha hates humans and no wonder. And I am sure Lucas and Noah think I am off my rocker." I was talking to myself.

"Samantha doesn't hate you or all humans." It was Grayson leaning against a tree. "And no one thinks you are off your rocker."

"How long have you been standing there?" Looking up at him.

He came down and sat beside me, "I was right behind you." Picking me up, he took my spot against the tree and sat me on his lap. "Samantha told me you left as soon as you were out the doors." He wrapped his arms around me.

With a sigh, I laid my head on his shoulder. "I thought I heard her, tattle tale." I smiled, taking another deep breath, "Grayson, what am I going to do?"

"What about?" He was hedging.

I sniffed, "You, Samantha, Lycans. You name it, I am out of my element here. Oh, and let's not forget my professor that has already tried to kill you, twice." I sounded pitiful, and I knew it.

He squeezed me, "Let's start with Samantha. She was taken by humans and held captive for ten years. But I don't think she has a hateful bone in her body." He moved one of his hands to massage the back of my neck again. "I will let her tell you the story when she is ready."

"And Rose?" I asked.

"Rose." He chucked, "She was taken captive too, but she was just a baby." Now he had moved his hand and was rubbing my back. "I doubt she remembers any of it."

I rested my hand on his chest, and his beast nudged it. "What about you?" I whispered, but I knew he heard me.

"Me?" He kissed the top of my head, "We are destined to be with one another." He answered. "Victoria, do I frighten you any longer?"

"No, not really. I know that you would never hurt me." I answered. "And other than on the plane, you have never raised your voice to me."

"That is true, and I am sorry about that." He apologized. I could tell he was thinking about something. "Did I frighten you when my Lycan started to emerge in front of your professor on the ferry?"

I sat up and looked into his eyes, "No, I don't think so. You were trying to frighten him and protect me from him."

His eyes never left my face, "So if I were to change into my Lycan form, I would not frighten you?" he asked.

His notion was becoming clear to me, tilting my head to the side I asked. "Can you tell me what happens first before you do? So I know what to expect."

"Of course." Looking me straight in the eyes, "You know about my eyes, they will change, glow, mine are red because I am an Alpha. Then, I will grow taller and stronger. Lycans are the strongest beasts in the other world." Seeing a question in my eyes, "We will cover that later. My body will contort as I am growing, and my hands and nails will look more like claws than what they look like now." He held out his hand for me to see his nails slowly extend.

I reached out and ran my fingers over his hand. "Is there more?" I asked.

"Yes, when I want. I can form into a wolf, just like the wild ones that roam free in these woods." He finished, "But even in my Lycan form or a wolf, I will never hurt you or let anyone or thing hurt you."

Just nodding that I understood. He lifted me off his lap and we stood. "I guess I should have started with this is easier when I am nude." He grinned then lifted his shirt over his head, then lowered his hands to the button and zipper of his pants.

When he reached for his pants, I stepped in front of him; "Can I?" I asked shyly.

Looking down at me, "You can do anything you want to me." I unbuttoned his pants and pushed them down over his hips. His cock was hard and standing straight out from his body.

"Oh," I whispered and reverted my eyes up to his face.

He just grinned, "That is what you do to me, Victoria. I can't help it." He kicked his boots and pants off then pushed me back and then started to grow and contort as he said. Though I know my eyes were wide as I watched, I was not afraid. "I'm still here, Victoria." His voice was deep, and I knew he was closer or in his Lycan form as he called it. He stood still; I knew deep down he was waiting on me to show him I was not afraid.

Stepping closer, I reached my hand up and stroked his chest, those red eyes looked down at me. There was tenderness in them. "You are beautiful," I whispered as I continued to stroke his chest. Then he contorted again, moving down to all fours as he transformed into a wolf. This time, he nudged my hand, and stroked his coat down his back, "So soft." I whispered. I knew Grayson was within, though I still didn't completely understand.

His head reached around, and he clasped his mouth around my wrist pulling me. I followed, he didn't run, just walked beside me as we came to a waterfall with a small lake. He walked into the water, and I watched as he came back to his human form. Reaching out his hand, "Victoria. Take your clothes off and come here." It was a quiet demand.

Chapter 11

Grayson

I just stood still and waited for Victoria to make up her mind. I would not rush her or force her. A moment later she nodded, there was a blush on her cheeks, but her eyes never left my face as she removed each piece of clothing. Once she was nude, she walked slowly toward me. At first, sticking only one toe into the water. "It's a little cold, but I will warm you up in a minute. Can you swim?" I asked.

"Yes, I was a ...." She smiled

Chuckling, "A Girl Scout? You told me that before, hopefully, they taught to swim better than they taught directions." By the time she got in front of me, her lips were quivering with cold. I just smiled and picked her up, "Wrap your legs around my waist." She did, leaning into me for warmth, I carried her out of the water and laid her down on the soft grass. Coming down on top of her. Having her nude under me was the sweetest torture I could imagine, I would not mate with her tonight, but I could give her pleasure. Her eyes were closed, "Victoria, look at me." I whispered.

She opened her eyes, there was a slight fear there. "Grayson are we going to...?" she asked.

"Mate?" I shook my head, "In two days will be the full moon. It is our tradition to mate for the first time under it, that is when I will claim and mark you as mine." I could see a question in her eyes, tilting her head to the side, "When we first mate, I will mark you." Running my fingers on the side of her neck, "Here."

Her heart was racing, "How?" she asked.

Letting my fangs elongate, "I will bite you." I watched as she nodded in understanding, "Then I will let a tiny bit of my blood flow into the wounds."

"Why?" She whispered.

Though I didn't mind teaching her about our ways, her naked body was a distraction. "I will tell you later." Moving down, I cupped a breast in my hand, letting my nails grow, I wanted her to learn and trust that I would not harm her. Then I leaned down and took her nipple in my mouth. "We may not be mating tonight, but I can give you something you have never had before." I suckled her, she moaned with pleasure. "Tell me what you like, Victoria," I said blowing on her hardened nipple.

Her eyes were closed to the new experience, "Again, please. Maybe a little harder." This time I let my fangs scrap across her nipple, "Yes, Grayson! I like that!"

"Good." I trailed my sharp nails down her stomach, to the trimmed patch of hair that covered the folds of her clit and pussy. Ever so slowly I ran a claw back and forth over her clit. "And Here?"

"Oh!, I...." She was breathing heavily. "Grayson? I want something." Moving down, I spread her legs.

I growled low, "I know what you need, mo chara." Then I lowered my head to feast on what I already knew would be the nectar of the gods. Victoria cried "Grayson!" surprised at my first lick.

Then arching her back she moaned; "Fuck! Yes!" She ran her fingers throw my hair pressing my face further into her cunt. "Grayson if you stop, I will die. I swear to God, don't you dare stop."

As I continued to lap at her cunt, I slowly inserted a finger, coming to the barrier of her virginity. Pushing slightly, I wanted to stretch her some before our mating. Hoping it would make it easier on her. When she cried out in pain, I retreated and continued to lick her back to the edge of an orgasm. It worked; she was moaning with pleasure again. "Grayson, what is happening to me?" There was wonder and a hint of fear of the unknown in her voice.

"It's okay Victoria. I am here, cum for me." I soothed between laps of all the nectar that was flowing from her cunt. "Let go! I will catch you!"

Her body became nearly ridged when she let go, "Grayson!" She screamed, I continued to lap at her as her pussy pulsed and convulsed. Slowly I brought her down to reality. Coming up I laid down beside her.

Wrapping her up in my arms, the night air was cool, and I knew she would get cold soon. She turned in my arms and laid her head on my shoulder. "WOW!" Coming up she looked into my eyes, "Is it always going to be that intense?"

I grinned as I trailed my fingers over her face brushing back her hair now tangled with grass. "I fully intend on making our mating as intense as you want."

Turning my head, I looked over to the left. "What is it?" she asked concerned.

Standing I stood to gather her clothes, "We need to leave, the wolves I told you about are coming for a nightly drink in the pond."

"Are they friendly?" I looked around.

I reached for her hand, "Not as friendly as I am." Leading her back to the clearing, one of the wolves followed baring his teeth, he snarled. Pushing Victoria behind me, I grew and showed my fangs, growling back. The wolf lowered his head and slowly backed away.

Victoria's hand was on my back, "What was that?" she asked.

When I turned there was no fear in her eyes. "He was just exerting his dominance. I just had to let him know I was the alpha here." Reaching down I grabbed my shirt and handed it to her. "This will cover you up until we get back to the house."

She looked down at the shirt, "I can't wear this back to Samantha's"

"We are not going back to Samantha and Lucas' the baby is probably asleep by now." She nodded slipping my shirt on then turned to the west and started to walk, I reached out and took her hand, pointing to the east. "That way." Chucking, "I am going to buy you a compass. Girl Scouts my arse!" Picking her up, "You will hurt your feet with no shoes on." Carrying her back to the house.

Victoria just wrapped her arms around my neck and laid her head on my shoulder. "Grayson? "Please put me down when we reach the grass. I don't want anyone to know that we were ....you know." She was adorable when she was embarrassed. I just nodded.

Chapter 12

Victoria

Even though Grayson agreed to put me down, he didn't, by the time we reached the grass I didn't care. I felt safe in his arms. I didn't get much of a chance to look around he just opened the front door of his house and carried me straight up the stairs to the bedroom kicking the door closed behind him.

I had not realized how tired I was, I watched as he stripped out of his pants and laid beside me, pulling me close. My eyes were closing as I rested my head on his shoulder, and he was covering the both of us up.

When I woke up, the sun was shining brightly through the windows. Grayson was gone, and I was nude. His shirt was on the floor, where he must have tossed it. I slipped it back on and tiptoed down the stairs looking for the kitchen. I came to an abrupt stop at the bottom stair, another man was facing Grayson as they talked. "Shit!" I murmured under my breath, turning to run back up the stairs.

"Victoria!" Grayson called out grinning from ear to ear at the sight of me. "This is Levi, I told you he could look at your computer for you." Thankfully his friend only called out his greeting and didn't turn around.

I peeked around the doorway, my cheeks had to be as red as a cherry! "Yes, Hello Levi." Glaring back at Grayson, "My computer is in my backpack. Excuse me, gentleman." I turned and dashed back up the stairs and hid.

Grayson came up a minute later, "You are so cute when you are embarrassed." I was not amused, looking around I grabbed a pillow and threw it at his head. Of course, he caught it in mid-air.

Slumping down on the side of the bed, "I didn't know you had company." I uttered.

Grayson came over and knelt in front of me. "Victoria." He lifted my face to look at him. "I am sorry, I should have come up and told you when I heard you moving around."

All I could do is sigh, "I am not used to being around so many men all the time." Looking over to my backpack, "Do you have a washing machine...I don't have any clean clothes with me."

Grayson just reached into his pocket and pulled out a cell phone and punched a number. "Hey, Samantha! Do you have some clothes Victoria can borrow? I will take her shopping this afternoon." Looking up at me he winked, "Great. Thank you." Returning his phone to his pocket. "She'll be over in a few minutes." Standing up, "Do you want some coffee or tea?"

Shocked at what he just did, "Just like that you are fixing all my problems?" I snapped my fingers. I shook my head, "You are going to have to allow me some independence, Grayson."

Standing I walked towards a bathroom, whispering, "I don't know, I just don't know."

Grayson stood to say something, but there was a knock on the door. "That is Samantha. I will send her up."

I just called out; "Sure, whatever. I am not allowed to have a thought in my brain." Turning on the water to the shower, I waited until the water was hot, then stepped in. The hot water did nothing for my mood. I was not sure what I felt. Smothered? Loved? I just didn't know. I scrubbed my head until it hurt, washing the rest of me. I knew I could not hide forever. Getting out, with a towel around me I stopped abruptly when I saw several pairs of pants and shirts had been laid out on the bed, along with bras and panties. Ashamed of my behavior, I lowered my head, she was just being nice. I need to apologize to her for last night, might as well add this one to the pile.

After getting dressed I went downstairs to find Samantha humming in the kitchen. Kelvin was crawling around on the floor. I could smell eggs and bacon, and my stomach grumbled. Samantha turned, "Oh good something fit!" Smiling up at me. "I am sorry I upset you last night."

Incredulous, "You upset me?" I uttered, "I should be apologizing to you. I brought back all those memories and then ran out. I am the one that is sorry." Looking down at the baby. "And thank you for the clothes." I looked back at her.

She walked over and placed a plate in front of me. "You are probably starving. Eat." Then she reached down and picked up the baby sitting across from me, holding him. He reached out for my plate, "No, Kelvin you had your lunch."

"Lunch? What time is it?" I looked around for a clock.

Samantha just smiled, "About twelve-thirty." Getting up at the sound of the tea kettle. She sat the baby back down, poured the hot water into cups, and placed a tea bag in each one. Bringing them back to the table she placed one in front of me.

Not believing I slept so late, "I never sleep this late. I am usually up around six."

She just patted my hand, "Not to worry. You have had a busy couple of days, and then there is jetlag." Looking down at her watch, "It is almost six thirty in the morning in Scotland. So, see you are right on time." Tapping her fingers on the table, "Now eat."

Not wanting to offend her, and I was hungry, I ate. "You sound just the opposite of my mother." I smiled and finished my breakfast. Standing I thanked her for cooking and went to wash up.

Samantha looked curious, "Why do I sound the opposite of your mother?" She stood and grabbed a dish towel as I washed, she dried the dishes.

Glancing over, I never really had a girlfriend I could confide in. "When I went to college I gained weight, and even more after she and my father got divorced." I could tell she didn't understand. "As I was gaining weight, she would tell me all the time, I would not find a husband if I was fat." Whispering the last word.

This time she was incredulous, "That is horrible!" She laid the dish towel down on the counter, "You are beautiful!"

"Yes, she is!" It was a growl from Grayson standing in the doorway holding Kelvin. Stepping into the kitchen. "Samantha" He handed her Kelvin. "I found this one in the study!" Sniffing, "I think he has a present for Lucas!" He grinned.

Taking her son, "Come on Kelvin, you are muddy and stinking up Uncle Grayson and Aunt Victoria's house." Walking towards the front door, she opened it calling back. "Just wait for your turn, Grayson!" Her laughter filled the air as she walked down the stairs.

Looking at the closed door, "You don't like children?"

Grayson just took my hand and led me to a laundry room. "Of course, I love kids. I just don't want to change one that isn't mine." Stepping back, "Here is the laundry room. You can wash anything you want."

Looking up, "I am sorry. I guess I have lived alone for so long I am just not used to having someone swoop in and fix my problems."

Crossing his arms over his chest, "I am a protector by nature, Victoria. But I promise I will TRY not to fix your problems before I talk to you." Grinning, "We will have to become accustomed to one another." Pushing away from the doorway, "Now why don't you make a list of what you need, and I will take you to town in about an hour." Shaking his head, "No, you cannot go by yourself. One, you will get lost. And two, your professor is still out there." He had raised a finger with each point.

Stretching up on my tiptoes, "See that was not so hard to explain, was it?" I smiled, "And who said I would get lost?"

Grayson just grabbed me for a long kiss, "I did. Girl Scout my arse!" We both wanted more, "I will meet you out front in an hour. I'm going to go check on the new trainees and get one of the SUVs" Reaching for the front door he turned looking severe, "Victoria, if you need me, call out I will hear you."

I went up to the bedroom and took out my dirty clothes from my backpack seeing my cell phone, I realized I had not spoken to my father or mother in some days. Looking around I grabbed Grayson's clothes to add to mine to wash. I had several messages, I started to listen to each as I walked back down the stairs with my arms full of clothes. Just as I dropped the clothes on the floor to sort through, the last message came through. *"Victoria, this is Professor Maxwell. I have your father, if you do not give me what I want I will not hesitate to kill him. Check your text messages for proof."* Then the line went dead. Looking down at my phone, there in my text messages were three pictures of my father bound and gagged, it looked like he had been beaten.

Tears were streaming down my eyes, if I tell Grayson he will be determined to save my father and get hurt or worse. But I don't have the information that Professor Maxwell is looking for, and that means my father will surely be killed. There was a knock on the door, not thinking I went and answered it.

"I wondered if...." It was Samantha, "WHAT'S WRONG?" There was a definite dread in her voice. I couldn't hide that I was crying.

With a deep breath, "You can't tell Grayson or Lucas!" I was insistent that she keep this from them. "My professor has my father and is threatening to kill him if I don't give him the information he wants." Handing her my phone, "It is the last message and there are text pictures of my father." I could not hold back the tears, "They beat him!" I cried.

Samantha looked down at the pictures, and then stepped up and wrapped her arms around me. "We have to tell Grayson and Lucas." She was patting my back, "They can help, this is what they trained for years for." Her voice was soothing as if she was talking to her son.

Sniffing, "I can't let Grayson get hurt again. I just can't." Still patting my back, the front door opened.

There stood, Grayson and Lucas, "What happened?" Grayson growled seeing my distress.

Samantha handed over my phone, "They or the Professor have her father." Still patting me on the back, "I think there is a voicemail too."

I raised my head, "There is." Grayson laid my phone on my outstretched hand; I punched the numbers so that they could hear the message. I walked into the living room; I didn't want to listen to it again.

Grayson came in sitting beside me on the sofa. "Why didn't you want to tell me?" I heard the front door close.

I looked over at him and sighed. "I don't want you to get hurt again, and I don't want my father to die." Looking out the window to the forest beyond, "How do I choose between you?"

Grayson scooted closer and picked up onto his lap. "You don't." Wrapping his arms around me, "Victoria, three hundred years ago, I was sent to train as a knight with the Order of Arcadia." Seeing that I was not quite understanding, "King Lycaon was the king of Arcadia, he was the first Lycan. Each one of us is a descendant of his, and the Knights that hid the treasure in the first place. We are duty bound to protect it." Lifting mp, "Lucas, Noah, Levi, and the others are all Knights of Arcadia, we can and will protect your father. And you are my mate, I will protect you."

"I don't want anyone to get hurt because of me." I tried to get up, but he held me tight.

Grayson pointed to a tapestry on the wall, "Do you see that?" Nodding, "It says *I promise on my life that I will in the future be faithful to the Order of Arcadia, never cause unnecessary harm, and will observe my homage to the Order completely against beings in good faith and without deceit.*' That is the oath we each took when we finished our training." Now he let me get up.

I looked at the tapestry then back to him, "But...."

Grayson placed my phone back in my hand, "Call the professor and tell him to bring your father here unharmed." His look and voice were intent and was not leaving me any room to argue.

With a small smile, "I don't know where HERE is." It was a simple statement, but he just grinned and wrote down what I needed to say. I called and demanded to speak to my father first, "Daddy, Are you okay?"

His voice was weak but clear, "I am okay Torie. I don't know what is going on, but ...."

Next, I heard the sneering voice of Professor Maxwell, "Satisfied? Now, where is my treasure?" I looked down at what Grayson had written and read, I heard Grayson shut the front door as he left. "No need to give me directions, I know where you are. See you in a minute."

'In a minute.' Rang in my head, he is close! I ran out the front door, I didn't see Grayson or Lucas. At the sound of gunfire, I looked down the road that we climbed last night. Not close, he is already here! I didn't think, I just ran across the courtyard and without knocking into Samantha's house. I yelled for her when I could not find her in the kitchen, dashing up the stairs, and continuing to yell. "Samantha!"

She came out of the nursery a little annoyed, "Victoria, I am trying...."

I reached for her hand, "You have to hide! Now!"

She could see the urgency in my eyes, then we heard more guns. "Kelvin!" Turning she picked up the baby from his crib, "Follow me." She held her son close to her chest as we went back downstairs to Lucas' study. She pushed a button under his desk and the bookcase opened. "Come with me, we will be safe down here." She urged.

I shook my head, "I can't. Grayson is out there and my father." Gently laying my hand on top of the baby's head, "You go." I whispered. "Be safe" I said as I pushed the bookcase back, I ran through the house and out the French doors. I heard someone kick in the front door. "Please god, keep Samantha and the baby safe." I prayed running around the corner of the house, there stood Professor Maxwell in the middle of the courtyard.

My father stood between two armed men, he looked over as I came within his site, "Where is my treasure? Victoria, I will not ask again."

Calling out, "It is here, let my father go, and I will show you." I prayed his greed would cloud the fact that I was lying threw my teeth. The professor turned and nodded to one of the gunmen. I watched as he raised his weapon and hit my father over the head, and he crumpled to the ground.

"You promised not to hurt him," I called out. Looking at my father unconscious on the ground. I had not seen Grayson or any of the others, Please God, don't let them be hurt. I prayed. "Follow me." I was thinking fast, where could I take them? THE WOLVES!

I started to walk to the forest, "Is this a trick?" He had caught up to me and grabbed my arm.

"No trick, it is hidden under the lake, by the waterfalls. This way." I continued to walk toward the forest only turning when I heard a growling behind us, then we saw at least five Lycans, engaged with the gunmen. Another had picked up my father and was carrying him to safety.

"Lycans!" The professor mumbled in disbelief at the site of the Lycan guards, then raising his gun he tried to shoot at the guards, yanking my arm free, I shoved him and turned. I had to find Grayson.

"Victoria!" Grayson roared! I closed my eyes just for a second, thank God, he was here. Turning I ran toward him, he was standing tall fully in his Lycan form. All six of them were there, standing shoulder to shoulder. Grayson stood in the middle; I knew him. And I kept running. Just then, everything slowed, and I felt a pinch in my back on the right side. I was only a few feet from Grayson as he ran to me, catching me as I slumped into his arms, whispering to him, "Mo Chara." The last sound I heard was a loud howl, then everything went blank.

Chapter 13

Grayson

"Victoria!" I roared. She pushed at the professor then turned and started to run toward me. I could see it in her eyes, she knew me from the others. Glancing up I saw the professor aim at her. She was too far for me or any of the others to get in front of her. I howled as she slumped against me. Picking her up, I called for Jackson to follow me, leaving Lucas and the others to deal with the professor.

Looking over as I came back to my human side, "She's been shot!" I took her into our home and carried her up to our bed laying her down on her stomach.

Jackson was already examining the wound and slightly turned her over. "The bullet when through her, but the blood is nearly black." Looking up at me with anguish, "I think it hit her liver. It isn't good Grayson I am sorry."

Fury ran through me, as I nearly tore off the bedroom door, "Stay with her!" I barked. But by the time I hit the front door I was back to my full Lycan form. "Where is he!" I roared! Turning I see Lucas, Noah, Wyatt, and Levi all striding toward me. They all knew I wanted to tear the professor limb from limb, and it would take all four of them to subdue me if needed.

"Grayson!" Lucas roared. He got my attention. In a stern voice, "Go take care of Victoria. NOW!"

All I could do was nod as I turned to stride back towards my home where I was afraid my mate was dying in our bed. I turned, "It's bad Lucas." I called over my shoulder, I could not hide the agony in my voice.

I heard Lucas giving orders, "Wyatt, you and Noah take Mr. Campbell to the human hospital. Make up a story as to how he got hurt." Turning, "Noah, bring back a human surgeon, I don't care if you have to drag one here."

I was up the stairs to see Victoria laying on her stomach again. "Tell me," I ordered.

Jackson just shook his head, "She's still alive, but I don't know." Looking down, "I can't see how bad it is without cutting her open." Then back to my face, "I have medical training, Grayson. But not for humans, I could kill her if I did."

Lucas was standing in the doorway, "I sent for a human surgeon."

Just then Victoria moaned. "Grayson?"

"Out!" I said to my friends. "Put some pants on please." Both Lucas and Jackson looked at each other and retreated out of the room. Victoria was trying to get up, "No, Victoria stay still." I whispered, placing my hand on her back to hold her.

"Grayson? Are Samantha and the baby safe?" Her voice was faint, but I heard every word. "They're in the bookcase."

Frowning, I finally understood what she was trying to tell me. "I will send Lucas to get them." Her eyes closed, and she was unconscious again.

"Lucas," I called out. "She must have gone and warned Samantha, she said they were in the bookcase." Looking down, "They are probably in the tunnels." Lucas just nodded and retreated from the room again. Jackson came back in wearing a pair of my pants, they hung off his hips, but I was happy he didn't go far.

Standing Jackson saw a wound on my hip. "Grayson, were you shot too?" Looking down to where he was pointing. "The bullet must have gone through her and hit you."

Walking into the bathroom, I was able to expel the bullet, the wound took only a moment to close. I grabbed a pair of pants and put them on. Taking the bullet, "It's silver." I handed it to Jackson.

Time seemed like it stood still when there was a commotion downstairs. Samantha was agitated. "I am going up to see her! Lucas, you are not stopping me." Her voice was deep, and she was growling. A moment later, the door opened, and Samantha ran to the bed where Victoria lay. Her voice was full of sadness, "I tried to get her to come in the tunnels with us." Looking up at me, "She came to warn me, I couldn't get her to come with me." She was crying and rambling, "I am so sorry, Grayson. I tried. She was worried about you and her father." Looking around, "Where is her father?"

Lucas was standing back in the doorway, "I had Wyatt and Noah take him to the human hospital. Noah is bringing back a surgeon with him." Just then we heard the sirens of an ambulance pulling up into the courtyard.

"Let me go!" A woman called out. Moments later, Noah strode in with a woman tossed over his shoulder.

"Here is the doctor." He set her down on her feet. "I took one of the ambulances too, just in case you needed... I don't know something from it." As he retreated, "Sorry, ma'am for the rough treatment, but as you can see it is an emergency."

The doctor turned and saw Victoria laying on the bed. "What happened to her?" Stepping forward, Samantha moved so she could see.

"She was shot, with this." Jackson handed her the bullet. "It went through her and hit Grayson in the hip. I think it hit her liver."

Looking around at all of us standing there, "I need to examine her, could I have some privacy please." When no one moved fast enough, "OUT!" She yelled.

Lucas, Samantha, and Jackson retreated from the room. "I'm staying." I insisted.

She just nodded, "I need to get her clothes off." Looking around, "Do you have any scissors?"

Not carrying what she saw, I extended a razor-sharp nail and sliced through Victoria's clothes, but she didn't seem afraid or shocked. "There are reasons we could not take her to a human hospital." I just stated. "You don't need to worry, no one here will hurt you."

Nodding, "I heard stories about all of you." Looking down at Victoria, "Your friend is probably right, this blood looks like it hit her liver. But unless she is bleeding internally, there isn't a lot of it." Looking up at me, "Is she your wife?"

I just nodded, letting her assume, I didn't want to explain our ways right now, "What does she need?" I asked.

Sighing, "The one that brought me here, I need some things out of the ambulance."

"Noah," I called out. He came in as I covered Victoria's naked body up. "The doctor needs some things from the ambulance, go with her, and help bring up what she needs."

Nodding, "Of course. Follow me, please." He stepped back from the doorway to let her pass.

They came back moments later, with arms laden with different medical items. "I'm going to start an IV to give her some fluids." The doctor explained. Victoria moaned.

Lean close to her ear, "I am here mo chara, lay still the doctor is here." I whispered.

Tilting her head to one side, "Mate?" Looking back to inserting the needle into Victoria's arm, "My grandmother was raised in Scotland, she taught me. "There." She said, as she placed tape to hold the port then on her other arm she put a wrap around and pumped a bulb, "I am taking her blood pressure." She continued to explain everything that she was doing. And placed earpieces in her ears, lifting a little metal disk, "So I can listen to her heart and lungs."

Nodding and appreciating the explanations, "Doctor, I am old. But I know the names of your medical supplies."

Nodding she looked up, "Mr. Grayson. I did find a portable ultrasound in the ambulance; I am just praying it works." Looking up, "I need to turn her over. I will do my best for her, but I can't promise anything."

When she reached for Victoria, I pushed her hands away, I gently turned Victoria over onto her back. As I watched she squirted liquid onto Victoria, "It helps the machine see what is going on inside." Looking up, "You may need to hold her down, I have to push to be able to see."

I called out for Jackson, "Hold her legs." As I braced my hands on Victoria's shoulders. I just nodded to the doctor to do what she needed.

Jackson was watching the monitor in wonder. Victoria tried to retch away groaning in pain. "She is in pain, how much longer!" I snapped.

She looked up, "I'm done." Pushing buttons on the monitor as I covered Victoria back up, "It looks like the bullet passed through just grazing the side of her liver." Pointing to the screen, "There." Standing up, "Even if I attempted surgery, I can't repair her liver. That's the bad news." Watching as Jackson leaves the room. "A blood transfusion might work, but it may not save her life."

Samantha was standing in the doorway, "What about Lycan blood?"

Lucas was behind her. "Samantha!" his tone was warming.

Looking at the doctor and then back up to me, "Grayson, our blood has healing powers. You could save her life by giving her your blood."

Lucas growled low, "Samantha it is against our laws, you know that." He warned again.

Samantha turned; "I don't care!" She growled back, "She probably saved my life as well as Kelvin's. Not to mention our unborn child." Placing her hand on Lucas' chest, "Kelvin is the heir to my father's title." A sob came from her throat, "She can't die, Lucas. She's my friend."

Lucas looked up to Grayson, "It has to be all of our decisions, agreed." I nodded.

"Lucas." I stopped him from walking out, he needed to understand. "I can't let her die. Even if they vote against it, I will give her my blood." I just nodded to let him know my decision. "If we have to live in hiding, I don't care, I will not lose her."

Lucas nodded and left, when the door closed, I extended my arm, making a fist, and a large vein popped up. "Do what you need to do," I ordered the doctor.

I could tell she was confused about what was just discussed. "I don't even know if you are the same blood type." She explained.

As I looked down at Victoria laying there, "Doctor, I am a Lycan. Victoria is human, we are fated, mates. Our blood will be compatible. As you heard, my blood has self-healing powers.

Please do what you need to give her my blood, or I will have Jackson come in and do it for you." Not wanting to waste any more precious time explaining, I was about to call Jackson in.

The doctor just nodded and started to insert a needle into my arm as Lucas returned. "We all agreed." Turning, "I am getting on the phone with the council, Liam and Fergus, to explain what has happened. I will call Murdoc too." I just nodded, my brother was the head of our clan and one of the Princes of Arcadia, I needed all the help I could get.

The doctor removed one bag of my blood, as she removed the needle, she placed a cotton ball over the tiny wound. "Hold that on there while I get a band-aid."

I just tossed the small cotton piece into the trash, "I don't need one." I said, then she turned and looked at my arm, there wasn't even a mark there.

Returning to Victoria, she fixed the bag of blood above her so that it could flow into her arm through the needle she placed before. "I hope you are right, or I just may have killed her." Looking around, she sat in a chair, "They will come looking for that ambulance."

I just nodded, "I will have Noah take you back to the hospital." I stood and held out my hand, "Thank you for coming. And, doctor, we all would appreciate it if you would not discuss what happened here. You can understand that we would be hunted down if humans knew of our existence here."

She shook my hand, "I understand, and I will be back." Thinking, "I will come up with some excuse as to why we took the ambulance." Looking back to Victoria, "I am off for the next few days, I want to stay with her to make sure she is going to be okay. With your permission of course."

"I would be most grateful." Then I called out to Noah. "Take the doctor and the ambulance back. And let the guards at the gate know that she will be returning."

I sat down in a chair beside our bed and watched as my blood slowly dripped into Victoria's arm, praying we were in time. No one could coax me to leave Victoria's side as she slept for days.

Chapter 14

Victoria

My eyes fluttered open; sunlight was peeking through the closed curtains. Turning my head, "Hello." A woman I didn't know said and smiled at me.

"Grayson?" I whispered.

He stood from a chair on the other side of the bed, "I'm here, Victoria." He looked worried. Standing he sat beside me on the bed. "How do you feel?" He gently brushed back my hair. The woman excused herself and left.

Tilting my head, "Fine actually. What happened?" Taking my hand he placed it on his chest, his beast nudged it. "He's worried." Thinking for a moment. "How do I know that?"

"Victoria, I need to tell you something." Grayson sounded worried. "The other day, when your professor attacked."

I thought back, "Grayson, MY FATHER! Is he?"

He took a deep breath, "He is fine, downstairs with Samantha and Kelvin." I looked towards the door. Turning my face back to him, "You were shot. And it was serious."

I looked him in the eyes, "I don't remember being shot."

"You were, and I had to give you my blood to save your life." His tone was serious, but I was not understanding what he was trying to tell me. "Victoria, I am a Lycan, we can self-heal."

Very slowly I understood what he was telling me, "You gave me your blood, so I could self-heal." At his nod, "Do you think I would be mad to be alive?"

He just shook his head, "I would hope that you would be happy to be alive." Looking me in the eye, "Lycans have other powers that may have transferred to you." Nodding, "You will no longer age as a human anymore. And you may be able to see in the dark and hear things that are a long distance away or whispered."

Inhaling, "There is someone on the other side of the door. I can smell them." I said in wonder. "Will I grow and contort into a Lycan like you?"

Lowering his head, "I don't know. It has been forbidden to transfer our powers to humans for more than a millennium."

Now I was worried, "Grayson are you in trouble for saving my life?"

He smiled as he looked back to me, "No, Lucas called the high council, Fergus and Liam explaining to them what happened. And my brother. That if not for you, Fergus' heir could have been killed, and the treasure lost."

"Who is Liam?" Turning my head towards the door. "My father is here," I whispered. "I could get used to this."

A light tap came, "Come in" I called out.

Tears were in my father's eyes as he advanced into the room, "Torie, my baby." Grayson got up and excused himself.

"Daddy." I patted the side of the bed. "How are you?"

"Me? Posh! I am fine. When that tattooed one brought me back here. They said you had been hurt and were un-conscious." He was patting my hand. "Even that doctor lady would not tell me what happened."

"I am fine daddy; I will be downstairs in soon." Still con-cerned, "They hit you on the head."

He reached up and tapped his head, "Only rocks up there. You know that." Looking around, "But I will tell you I had some strange visions there for a moment, I thought." Leaning back, he sighed "Just this old man's mind playing tricks on me. Not to worry. But you, how do you feel? That Grayson has been hovering over you night and day."

All I could do is pat his hand, "I am glad you are all right daddy." Grayson tapped on the door and came back in.

"Sir, the doctor wants to check on Victoria." He stated. Stepping out of the doorway so my father could pass.

Patting Grayson on the chest. "My baby is going to be fine." He sniffed. Grayson looked down to his chest with his brows furrowed and then watched as my father descended the stairs.

I just giggled, "He likes you. I can tell." Pushing myself up to sitting, Grayson moved to help me, but I just waved him off, continuing. "He is thinking of you as the son he never had."

Still incredulous, "I'm over four centuries older than him." Grayson looked at me and back to the stairs.

"I'm not going to tell him that are you?" I folded my arms over my chest.

With a boyish grin, "No, I don't suppose I am." Grayson walked over to the bed sitting back down, "You scared the shit out of me, Victoria." Taking a hold of my hand. Grumbling, "Don't do that again."

All I could do is smile, as I pulled my hand free stroking his chest until I felt his beast nudge me, "I promise." I smiled.

"May I come in?" There was a tap on the door, and the woman that was here earlier stepped in.

Grayson stood, "Yes, of course. Victoria this is Dr. Melissa Herbert. Noah insisted that she come to help you. And she has been tending to you since." He winked and grinned as he walked out.

She just smiled, shaking her head, as she walked over to the bed. "There is a story in there somewhere." I hinted. She took my wrist and was looking at her watch.

"Oh, he kidnapped me, stole an ambulance, and threw me over his shoulder to get me up here." Looking up at me she nodded, "Your pulse is good." Then she pulled a pen light and looked into my eyes. "How do you feel?"

Looking left and right as she asked. "Fine."

She put her stethoscope in her ears and listened to my breathing. "He has barely left your side." Nodding towards the door. "I can only hope I find a man that cares for me that much one day." There was a wistfulness in her voice. Tugging at my shirt, "May I?" Lifting my shirt, we both looked down to see only a slight mark under my right breast. Leaning forward, she looked at the area where the bullet entered my body. "Barely a mark. You were lucky."

"Thank you, doctor." I knew Grayson was on the other side of the door waiting to get back to me. "Grayson, you can come in," I called out.

He walked in and winked at me, nodding to the doctor. "Is she good?"

Looking up at his worried face and back to mine, "I would say, she is completely healed." Turning back to me, "But please do not overdo it for a few days." Looking back to Grayson, "You can make sure she doesn't do too much for a few days."

There was some sense of relief on his face, "I can." Looking at me, "She will rest, I promise."

Not wanting to argue in front of the doctor, I just nodded. But I could tell by the way Grayson was looking at me, I would barely be allowed out of this bed much less out of the house if I let him have his way.

That night, Grayson was sitting in the chair in the room, reading my research notebooks. "Grayson? What happened to the professor?"

Chapter 15

Grayson

When she asked about the professor, I growled with anger and frustration but calmed myself. Then I answered Victoria, "He is alive." I grumbled, "The high council decided a punishment for him was to let him only see a treasure, but never be able to touch it for the rest of his days."

Not understanding, "You mean he is still here?" She asked and I nodded, I still would prefer to tear him limb to limb, but I had to respect their decision was out of my hands.

When I nodded she exclaimed, "He should be in prison."

She deserved the truth, so I explained, "In a way he is. We have him in one of our cells in the tunnels where there is an image of a treasure that is beamed onto the wall." I could tell she was tired and didn't understand what I was saying. "He will only be able to look at the image for the rest of his life. We will feed him, but he will never be able to get out of that cell or touch the treasure."

She whispered, "You are driving him mad." Then she thought and said, "A treasure, but not The treasure."

Grinning not much gets past her, I nodded and stood, "You are tired, Victoria. Please rest as the doctor said." Kissing her forehead as I walked to the door, "I will see you in the morning." There was a look of disbelief on her face, and I knew she would get up. The moment I closed the door, I heard the rustle of the covers as she tossed them off of her, and the slightest sound of her feet as they touched the floor, "Get back in bed, Victoria!"

She muttered, "Damn his Lycan hearing." But she did as I said and laid back down, I stood outside our bedroom leaning against the wall listening until her breathing evened out into a deep sleep.

I remember the days that followed Victoria being shot. Still in a rage and frustrated that I could not take his life. But I would not leave her side for fear, she would never wake up, Lucas had online meetings and discussions about what should be done with Professor Maxwell and his gunman. But they also discussed in length what should happen to me and Victoria.

There were a few of the High Council that wanted me stripped of my knighthood and banished from Lycan society. One even suggested that Victoria be taken to a Lycan compound to be watched over to see if she had fully been turned into a Lycan herself.

When I heard that they may try to take her away from me I walked out to the woods and howled in rage as I destroyed several trees before I calmed down. Lucas had followed me out, leaning against a still-standing tree, "Feel better now?" He asked.

Growling, I walked past him and barked, "They are not taking her away from me, Lucas." It wasn't a plea it was a statement.

He nodded, "I won't let them." Then he explained as we walked back to my house,

Our one saving grace was Eryn, Lucas told me. He appeared at one of the meetings and said that if Victoria was turned, we are lucky to have her in our world. Not only that but she saved the heir to Fergus' title and estate. Another point he made was that Liam had yet to find a mate and had no heirs of his own that now Kelvin was the heir to be the next Prince of Arcadia.

Liam was not happy to be reminded of his situation, but Lucas said that he accepted the truth.

Chapter 16

This is how my life was for weeks, Grayson would not let me out of bed. Even refused to let Samantha visit, saying I was resting. In those weeks, my father left to go home, and Lucas had him flown back to California on the plane, escorted by four Lycan guards. Grayson would not permit me to go and see him off, but my father, kissed me goodbye, whispering, "You have a good man there Torie." Then I watched as he walked out my bedroom door.

The final straw was when for the hundredth time, Grayson tried to follow me to the bathroom, "I have been doing this by myself for several years!" I slammed the bathroom door closed in his face. Determined not to go back to bed, I showered, got dressed, and came downstairs. Grayson was lifting a tray to bring up to me for lunch. "I am going to go see Samantha!" I announced. Looking back over my shoulder, "And don't you dare follow me, Grayson Sinclair!" I growled low.

When I stepped off the porch and headed towards Samantha's house, I could feel his eyes watching me from the front porch. "Don't you have something better to do, Grayson?" I uttered, but I knew he heard me.

Lucas answered the door when I knocked. There was a surprised look when he saw me, then he looked back over to our house. "Is Samantha home?" I asked sweetly as I entered the house. Then turning to look back Grayson was walking toward me, "Lucas, take him somewhere, and do something with him. He is driving me crazy!"

Samantha emerged from the kitchen, "Victoria, what a pleasant surprise!" she exclaimed with a big smile as she came up and hugged me.

I gave her a weak smile and walked into the kitchen; "Before you ask. I feel fine." I slumped down onto one of the kitchen chairs, I heard the front door close. "Samantha, I don't know what to do."

Setting an empty cup in front of me, "Tell me what is going on." She moved back to the stove and put the tea kettle on a burner. Coming back to the table, she sat down across from me. "Grayson keeps telling me you are resting as the doctor ordered. I am surprised you are here."

All I could do is sigh, "Yes, she told me to rest for a couple of days. It's been weeks." Shaking my head, "She came to check on me yesterday and was also surprised I was still in bed. Grayson is driving me mad!" The tea kettle started to whistle, and Samantha got up. "That's not the worst of it."

As she poured the water into our cups. "What could be worse?" she asked.

"Is Lucas here?" I knew that even whispering he could hear me if he were in the house. Samantha just shook her head no. "We haven't..." Looking down in the darkening water, "...you know." I was desperate for some advice. "I want to…" Even talking to Samantha about this was embarrassing.

"Mate?" She uttered. Looking directly at me, "You want to mate, and he won't? Is that what you are trying to say?"

Relieved that she understood, "Yes." Looking her straight in the eyes, "Before I was shot, he kissed me and would say things to me about …mating all the time. Now, nothing. He won't even sleep in the same room with me." Sighing again, "He treats me like I am going to fall dead if he touches me that way. Maybe he no longer desires me." I sounded miserable and pitiful.

Samantha sipped her tea, "Nonsense. He was afraid that you were going to die, we all were." Thinking for a moment, "After he gave you his blood, you remained unconscious for days. It scared us all." It was her turn to take a deep breath, "But as you say you are fine now."

"Do you have any ideas how I fix this?" I urged for any help she could give me.

She looked up, "Kelvin is awake." Rising from the table, "You stay there I will get him and think."

As she walked up the stairs, I heard the front door open, standing I came around the corner to see Lucas and Grayson coming in. "Grayson Sinclair, I am perfectly fine and need some time alone. Please!" I pleaded. I had not yelled, but I knew he heard the desperation in my voice. "Lucas, please tell Samantha I said thank you for the tea, but I am going for a walk. I need some fresh air."

Before I could walk past Grayson, "Victoria?" he whispered.

"Not now Grayson, please." Whispering back. I walked out the door, down the steps, and across the courtyard to our house.

Chapter 17

Grayson

Victoria sounded so defeated. *Did I do this to her?* I wondered as I stared after her. I was just about to go after her when Samantha's voice stopped me. "Grayson, do you have a moment to help me in the kitchen, please?"

Lucas just shrugged his shoulders when I looked over at him. "Yes, of course." I turned and followed Samantha to the kitchen.

Samantha stepped up to me and handed me little Kelvin, "Can you put him in his highchair? You will need the practice for when you and Victoria have young of your own." I did as she asked and made sure that the baby was secure.

"Is there anything else? I need to go and check on Victoria." I said and started to leave.

She just shook her head, "Victoria is fine for a few minutes. Grayson, please sit down." Though she was smiling I knew something was up. I would not offend her, so I sat. "Thank you." Sitting across from me, she started to feed Kelvin. "Victoria is upset. She looked over at me.

I just nodded, "And you know why, don't you?" I uttered.

As she put another spoonful of food in Kelvin's mouth, "She needed someone to talk to." Smiling at her son as he ate, "Grayson, are you afraid she is still going to die?"

All I could do is smile; Samantha was acting as a mother hen for Victoria. "I know she has healed, but..."

She tilted her head to one side, "But, what? Your blood worked; she healed." Turning she gave Kelvin another spoonful of food. "But Grayson, even though Victoria may have some of our powers now, she is still a human woman inside with human feelings."

"What are you trying to tell me?" I wasn't sure where this conversation is going.

Samantha stood and got a washcloth and whipped the baby's face, "All done!" She smiled and then turned to me. "I am pretty sure that Victoria is in love with you. And you are blowing it."

I just shook my head, "We are fated to be together, that is all she is feeling. And I failed to protect her."

She looked confused, "Lucas told me what happened, none of you could have gotten in front of her in time. She was too far away."

The memory of that day flooded back in my mind and even though I knew what Samantha was saying was true, I still felt as if I failed to protect Victoria from getting shot. "Samantha,

I appreciate you trying to help." I stood to excuse myself and leave.

"Grayson, is this the reason you have not mated with her?" She whispered.

I turned and looked at her, "She told you." I was incredulous that Victoria would speak of something so personal.

Samantha nodded, "She needed a female to talk to. And she thinks you no longer desire her." Stepping up to me she patted my arm, "You need to fix this Grayson." She advised.

She was right. I needed to fix this, but how? As I started to walk back to our house, I suddenly turned and headed for the woods. Now I needed some time to think.

I was at the clearing, pacing around. It was now dark, I had been out here for hours, and nothing was coming to me. It was time I headed back home. Just as I cleared the line of trees, a feeling of warmth swept over me, Victoria was my home.

As I walked into the house, I could see that Victoria was sitting on the back porch, wrapped up in the kilt I had given her. I heard a sniff; and watched as she whipped her eyes, she has been crying. Trying to be as quiet as I could, "I heard you come in." She called out.

All I could do is just smile, "Are you warm enough?" I asked. She turned her head and her eyes flared with anger.

Then she took a deep breath, "Yes I am fine, thank you for asking." There was still a hint of defeat in her voice.

Now I knew I had a problem on my hands if she was not arguing back at me. "Victoria." I knelt in front of her, "I am sorry I have been treating you like a porcelain doll these last few weeks." I reached out my hand.

She looked at my outstretched hand, "I'm not going to break, Grayson." Insisting and instead of taking my hand she reached out and trailed her fingers over my face. "I healed, because of you." Her voice was warm and tender.

I could not look away from her, "And you were hurt because of me." I stated.

She just shook her head, "How so? Samantha told me what happened that day. I was too far away from anyone of you to get to me." Smiling, "Grayson you are strong and undoubtedly fast. But you are not faster than a speeding bullet. None of you are Superman." She had trailed her fingers down to my chest where my beast was nudging her hand.

I wanted her in my arms, standing I picked her up and sat down where she had been with her on my lap. "There, now tell me who is the Superman person," I growled in her ear, teasing I knew who the fictional character was.

She turned to look into my eyes, "No one important." Victoria leaned closer to me, "Grayson, I need."

As I threaded my fingers through her hair and brought her mouth to mine, "I know mo chara." Our kisses were ravenous and not enough, my beast was restless to get out, "Claim her!"

She pulled back from me, "Did you just say something?"

Her hand came from around my neck to my chest, "You heard my beast." I grinned.

Unbelievably her eyes glowed yellow with desire, as she blushed. "He is impatient."

Holding her hand to my chest, "We both are." Kissing her lightly, "The moon will be full tomorrow, Victoria." It was a low growl of my desire to make her mine at last.

She just grinned, "It's about fucking time!" Wrapping her arms around my neck again, she pulled me to her and kissed me with the hunger we both felt.

As hard as it was, we managed to tear ourselves away from one another. But I was not going to stay away from her again this night. Victoria was climbing into bed, and I strode into the room. She watched with growing desire as I stripped and climbed in beside her, "Never again, will we sleep apart." I grumbled.

She just giggled and snuggled into my awaiting arms, "That wasn't my idea."

Morning came, and I needed to keep myself busy until it was time to claim her. Just as I was about to walk out the door to head for the training fields, Victoria called out. "I am going to see Samantha."

She didn't sound upset, but I wondered what that was about.

Chapter 18

Victoria

I walked across the courtyard to Samantha's. I knew Grayson was confused, we had talked and settled so much last night. There was a pulling in me when I woke up this morning. It was like the full moon that was going to rise this evening was calling me, and I could not resist it. On top of that, I was a bundle of different emotions, excited, scared, and happy, I just could not put a finger on how I felt. Coming up to their front door, I knocked and greeted Lucas when he answered. "Good morning, Lucas, is Samantha home?"

Samantha came around the corner from the kitchen, smiling, "I see you two worked things out. I hope." Lucas stepped back as I came in and walked out the door closing it behind him.

"Yes," I uttered, looking around, thankful that Lucas left I just could not bring myself to have an awkward conversation with him being able to hear.

She just smiled, "Have you had breakfast?" I just shook my head, looking around, I sat at the table, then jumped up walking around pacing I sat again when she looked again and fidgeted in my seat.

Calmly, Samantha came over and covered my hands, with one of hers. "Victoria, you are jumpy as a rabbit, tell me what's wrong, please." She smiled, "You and Grayson did talk things through last night?" It was a question, but there was concern in her voice.

My eyes popped up to hers, "Oh, yes." Nodding, "It's just I am nervous about ..."

"Mating." Her voice was calm, but she smiled. "Didn't your mother ever talk to you about sex?"

Rolling my eyes, "Yes," I was exasperated, "She said 'Good girls don't do that until they are married." Lowering my head, "That was the end of the conversation."

"And your father never..?" She trailed off.

My head snapped up and my eyes were big as saucers, "Oh god NO!" Then I chuckled. "He almost died of embarrassment when I had my first period. And had to go get me pads."

She laughed, "Yeah, I think my father hid from me during my first one." Standing she walked over to the stove and cracked a couple of eggs into a pan. Looking over her shoulder, "Do you need to know what is going to happen?"

Sighing, "Yes and no. I mean I know the mechanics of sex. Even though I am a virgin. Looking down at my hands, "I just don't know how Lycans do things."

She turned to lift the pan and put the eggs on the awaiting plates, "We are not so much different than humans, Victoria."

Coming over to the table, she sat the plates down, and we ate. "Lycans like to chase their prey." She said finally. Getting up she took our plates and headed to the sink.

I stood and followed Samantha, grabbing a dish towel to dry the dishes as she washed them. "Chase?" I whispered.

She turned her head and grinned. "Yes, Chase." Then her grin got wider, "The first time we mated Lucas chased me into the woods." she had handed me the last plate, as she spoke. Then stopped blushing she shook her head no.

After I dried the plate I put it in the cabinet, then nudged her with my shoulder, "Oh come on, Samantha. I don't have anyone else to talk to." My cheeks felt flush, and a stirring of excitement hit me when she said 'chase'.

She looked around to make sure we were alone, then up to the ceiling, making sure little Kelvin was asleep still. Taking my hand, we went into the large living room and sank on the sofa facing a fireplace. "Chasing their mates before mating excites male Lycans." She was whispering and still blushing. "I bathed and prepared myself for the first time we were going to mate."

"And?" I coaxed her to continue.

"Only dressed in his robe, came downstairs here and walked out the doors." She smiled, "When I got to the grass, I ran. Lucas came after me. He chased me." She turned at the sound of the front door.

Lucas and Grayson came in, "What are you two talking about?" Lucas asked with a raised eyebrow. Grayson was right behind him with his arms folded across his chest.

"Girl talk" "Sex" Samantha and I blurted out at the same time. Then looked at each other and started to laugh.

"Well, which is it?" He chuckled.

Samantha stood and walked over to Lucas, patting him on the chest, "Girl talk." Then she mimicked his stance, "What are you doing here?"

Lucas leaned down kissing her nose, "I live here." Then he quickly caught her up in his arms, growling into her ear. "Later, mate."

Blushing to the roots of my hair, I walked over to Grayson, "Let's leave them be, I want to start dinner."

"Dinner, it's not even lunchtime yet," Grayson growled. I just shook my head and rolled my eyes at him. Then he grinned, "Oh, yes we need to start dinner." He called out as he shut their door. Hand in hand we walked across the courtyard to our home.

Chapter 19

Grayson

Victoria is so beautiful when she blushes. When we got home this morning, she let go of my hand and went straight up to our room, and I have not seen her since. Honestly, I left soon after, when she blurted out that she and Samantha were talking about 'sex' that word went straight to my cock. And visions of her spread out underneath me naked have played over in my mind all day keeping me hard as a rock. My concentration was so bad that a couple of the recruits were able to knock me on my arse out in the training field.

Thankfully the sun had begun to set, and the full moon was coming up. Instead of going home to get cleaned up, I went to Levi's. I didn't ask, just knocked and grumbled I needed to use his shower and walked upstairs. Now clean, I quietly stepped into our home, Victoria was sitting out on the back porch wrapped in the kilt I had given her. "Mo chara," she whispered without turning her head. And for the first time, I could see that her eyes glowed yellow as she looked out to the dense woods beyond.

"Victoria?" Afraid that this change would frighten her, I stepped closer.

Turning her head, there were tears, in her eyes, whispering almost in reverence, "I can see so much, Grayson." Then she looked back out to the woods, pointing. "Look there. A rabbit."

Training my sight to where she pointed, "I see him." I crouched down beside the chair she sat in, "Are you okay?"

She turned and looked at me, it was then I realized Samantha was right. I could see the love in her eyes, as she reached up and caressed my face, "I am fine. It is just so beautiful." Waving her hand out to encompass everything around her, "I never knew."

Standing I reached for her to put her on my lap, but she shook her head, "No, you will ruin my surprise."

My eyebrow shot up, "Surprise? For me?" Crouching back down, so I could look her in the eye.

She blushed and nodded at the same time, "Samantha told me Lycan males like to chase their mates." She looked down then back up into my eyes. "Do you want to chase me, Grayson?"

Victoria had no idea what she was doing to me, "More than you could possibly know." I growled low.

The fingers that were caressing my face moved down my chest and abdomen. Her eyes followed her fingers, "When she told me that, I got.." she trailed off.

"Aroused?" I offered to finish for her. She smiled and nodded.

Now looking up at the full moon, "Is it time?" she asked.

Determined to make this night perfect I was not going to rush her, "If you want it to be." I said. With a quick nod, she moved her feet out of underneath her, and stood, that is when I noticed her feet were bare. Inhaling, I could smell her arousal.

She turned and whispered with a grin on her face, "Don't follow me right away."

She walked down the steps that led to the lawn, leading out to the woods, I watched as she stood for just a moment, glancing over her shoulder her eyes flashed then she ran into the woods.

Standing I reached down and removed my boots, then pulled my t-shirt over my head. My beast was anxious to chase after her, but I wanted to give her a minute to run. Slowly I walked down the three steps to the grass, my eyes never leaving her. She was weaving in and around trees. Her new ability to see in the dark made it easier for her to see which way she was going. Not able to resist her any further, I ran after her. "Victoria, I am coming for you," I growled.

Her laughter filled the air, "You have to catch me first, Grayson."

She was enjoying our game, and I knew I could have her in a few steps, my stride was longer than hers, and I was faster. But I kept my pace slow, to let the anticipation build in each of us. Wanting to direct her toward the lake I weaved around some trees, instinct had her going exactly where I wanted to catch her. When she dropped my kilt, my breath hitched at the sight of her naked body as she ran. Not stopping I grabbed the kilt as I pursued her.

"You are mine, Victoria!" I howled. All I needed was three steps and I had her around the waist. Scooping her up in my arms, she turned to me, smiling and panting from her exertion.

"Now that you caught me, what are you going to do to me?" Her tone was teasing, but I could see the desire in her eyes.

The memory of what I told her on the plane came to mind, so I repeated it. "Victoria, I am going to fuck you all night under this full moon. I am going to lick up all those sweet juices I can smell dripping from your cunt. And you are going to moan and scream with pleasure as I thrust my cock in you."

Smiling her mouth was just a breath from mine. "Promise?"

Grasping her head with one hand, I captured her mouth for a long and ravenous kiss. When I pulled back, her eyes glowed even as she panted for breath, and her voice was deep when she demanded "More."

Coming down to my knees, I laid her down on the soft grass, "Mo Chara, I am going to give you so much more, you will have trouble walking for the next couple of days." Grinning, I trailed kisses from her mouth down her neck until I reached her breast, leaning in I licked her hardened nipple then took it in my mouth sucking. As I worshiped her nipple, my fingers trailed to the other breast cupping it in my large hand. Moans of pleasure escaped Victoria. I released her nipple from my mouth glancing up to look at her face. Then I took the other nipple in my mouth.

Her hands reached up as her fingers threaded around my head, "Grayson, that feels so good." Smiling at her admission.

Releasing her breast, my hand trailed down her abdomen, to the trimmed hair that covered her clit. "It's only going to get better, mo chara." My mouth had followed my fingers and now was just at her rosy swollen bud, inhaling, I looked up at her face, "Your scent is intoxicating, and I remember the taste of your nectar."

She gasped when I let my tongue glide over her slick folds and clit. "Grayson!" moaning. I placed my hands under her wrapping around her thighs to hold her still, as I intensified feasting on her. Nectar flowed from her cunt all over my mouth and beard. Slowly I inserted a finger and started to fuck her with it. Hooking the tip slightly so that I could rub the spot just right. She pushed at my shoulders, at the building feelings, and then changed to holding my head to her pussy. Keeping my pace, I slipped in another finger, my cock twitching at the feel of her tight cunt surrounding them. *Claim her!* my beast growled.

Her body was tight and I knew she was close to exploding. "Cum for me, Victoria," I whispered. "Let go, I will catch you."

My shoulders stung as her nails dug in with her tight grip, "Grayson!" she screamed as she toppled over the edge into oblivion, but I didn't let up my pace until her body stopped convulsing, only then did I slowly bring her back to reality. Standing quickly, I removed my pants, Victoria watched as my cock bounced and stood straight out from my body.

Wrapping my hand around my shaft, I stroked. Victoria came up to her knees to watch a small smile play over her face, "Fondle your breasts for me, Victoria," breathing hard as if I had run miles uphill as I stoked faster, but she did as I commanded. "Pinch your nipples," I growled. Her eyes flashed, with excitement. "Come closer." She moved close to the tip of my cock, and the tip of her tongue escaped her mouth as she licked the precum that dripped from my cock. The sight put me over the edge, "Open your mouth." With one hand I gripped her head and bought her mouth over my cock, the other hand continued to stroke. "I am going to cum, Victoria, swallow it all." Releasing my cock, I held her head still as I moved in and out of her mouth with the last few strokes. When my first release hit, I threw back my head and howled, and continued to pump into her mouth.

Victoria smiled when I pulled my cock from her mouth, "I liked that!"

When she reached out to grasp my shaft, I pulled her hand away, "You can have more later," I growled smiling at her enthusiasm. Then I came down, laying her back down. Spreading her legs to accommodate my size, the tip of my cock was right at the entrance of her cunt, looking down into her eyes, I twitched slightly. "Are you still afraid Victoria?"

She shook her head 'no' as she whispered, "A little," realizing her contradiction her smile widened. "I am, but I know you will make it all right." Her hands were stroking up and down my arms, and I could feel the love pausing through her gentle touch.

Leaning forward I lightly kissed her lips, letting the head of my cock enter her. "I will go slow, to let you get used to me." Her arms wrapped around my neck as I pulled back and slowly pushed back into her a little more. My beast was pacing with the desire to slam into her, but she was so tight, I pushed him back. Taking my time going deeper with time, stopping only when I was fully embedded in her. I watched her face for any signs of pain as I went deeper and deeper. Leaning down, kissing her lips, "Can you feel me, Victoria?"

Stretching up, she kissed me, "You have filled me." Then a wicked smile came across her face, "Now what?"

Chuckling, "We have just begun," I pulled back and with a little more force, I delve back into her. Coming back almost immediately, repeating my action.

Moaning, Victoria's back arched and she wrapped her leg around my hip. "Grayson, I feel like, it is going to happen again."

"Cum for me Victoria!" I growled making my pace faster, then moving my hand to encircle her clit. Her body was tight as a bowstring.

The feel of her cunt convulsing over my cock had me running to the edge myself, and letting go, my cum filled her cunt full. I pulled out and quickly flipped her onto her knees. My beast was coming to the surface, and I growled, "Watch me, Victoria," I thrust back into her, and she turned and looked over her shoulder as my beast came forth.

Growling, "Mine!" He leaned over her and turned her head, revealing the spot where she would carry our mark for all time. "You are ours, Victoria." He growled again, then licked her neck just before we sank our fangs into her. Pulling back, I came back halfway to my human form and let my fangs sink in again, then biting the inner side of my lip, my blood flowed into the wound to mingle with hers. Looking down at our joined bodies, could feel her body tighten again, "Can you cum for me again?"

Her answer was to throw her head back, growling my name as her body convulsed around me, bringing me to my release. Slowly I pulled out of her, proud that she was now completely ours. I moved and laid down bringing her to my side.

It was almost like I could feel her thinking, and I could not wait until she had gathered her thoughts. "Grayson?"

Her hand was stroking my chest, "Yes," I said kissing her head.

"Will you always bite when we.." she could not finish her question.

"Mate?" I offered. At her nod, "No, but I can if you want me to." Answering.

"Maybe I will let you know. Okay?" I nodded, and I could tell she had not finished with her questions. "Don't I get to bite you?"

It took me a minute to figure out what she meant. "You mean claim me?"

"Yes, that is what I mean." She whispered.

Not wanting to offend her, "That isn't how it works." I squeezed her tighter to me. "I am the male, and the male marks his female."

She snorted, "That seems a little sexist to me." Then she patted my abdomen, "You Lycans need to get with the times, Grayson."

I rolled over pinning her under me, "I am the male, Victoria." I growled.

Her small hand trailed down my body, slowly wrapping her fingers around my shaft, she grinned, "You most certainly are." She spread her legs and guided me to her entrance. Smiling, "I think I am still able to walk, you have your work cut out for you."

Growling at this little female of mine, I pushed into her. "Say the words, Victoria."

Her eyes came to mine, even as she moaned with pleasure, "I am yours, Grayson."

Chapter 20

Victoria

Last night Grayson claimed me, I was looking in the mirror of our bathroom, and turned my head to inspect the mark on my neck. We stayed out by the lake until dawn, and as he calls it mated several times. Though I am still able to walk, I am sore. But it is a satisfying sore. I never thought that I would scream with so many orgasms, it was a wonder I didn't have a sore throat as well. Turning from the mirror I peeked into the bedroom, then started a hot bath.

Sinking into the steaming water, helped my sore muscles, and the tenderness between my legs. Enjoying the luxury of the bath, I soaked until the water was nearly cold, getting out. Last night when I prepared to run out into the woods, I realized that Grayson didn't have a robe, so I used the kilt he gave me. I needed to do laundry again, we never made it to go shopping, and I have not gotten my things from my apartment yet, so I opted to borrow one of his t-shirts. It hung down to my thighs and looked more like a dress, but that was fine. Slipping on some clean panties, I tip-toed out of the bedroom and headed down to the kitchen.

Getting a pot of coffee started I was leaning against the counter, looking out to the courtyard. I heard Grayson moving

"

around upstairs and got down two cups. Then he appeared in the doorway, gorgeously nude, growling he stalked toward me, "Why are you not in bed?" Not giving me a chance to answer, he grabbed me, tossed me over his shoulder, and carried me back upstairs, "You are tired, and should be sleeping. WITH ME!" He stressed the last part.

Putting me down on my feet, he stripped me of his shirt, then reached for my panties. "I get it," I lowered my panties down, then kicked them over to where he threw his shirt. Then I climbed back into our bed and waited for him to join me.

Once he was settled, with me against his side, "How do you feel this morning?" he asked with concern.

Not about to lie to him, "I am sore. But the bath helped." Then I could not resist, "But as you can see, I can still walk," I giggled.

Rolling over and pinning me under him, "You are lucky to have such a thoughtful mate, that you can walk today." Then he kissed my nose as he ordered. "Go back to sleep."

Snuggling closer to him, I rested my head on his chest, the rhythmic beating of his heart put me back to sleep. Not sure of the time, I stretched awake. Grayson was gone, and I was hungry. Putting back on my panties and his t-shirt, I went back downstairs. He was standing against the counter, with just his jeans on sipping on a cup of coffee. I walked up to him smiling and stretched up on my tiptoes kissing his mouth. A growl emanated from him, as he laid down his cup and pulled me tighter to him, lifting me and kissing me hard.

I wanted more, and he knew it but refused to take me back upstairs. "You are sore, Victoria."

Smiling, "I am tougher than I look," whispering as I trailed kisses down his neck.

"You will regret it. If I take you back upstairs." He growled into my ear.

Pulling back, "Why upstairs, these granite counters look pretty steady to me." Grinning.

His eyes widened then he turned and sat me down on the counter. "Lift your hips," he demanded. When I did he slipped my panties down my legs, then knelt in front of me. "I know what you need."

Widening my legs, I leaned back when his hot breath blew on my clit. "Stop teasing." I moaned out my demand, then boldly pulled his face to my cunt. He didn't hold back, licking and sucking. I had placed my foot up on his shoulder, exposing myself to him more. That wonderful feeling was beginning to spread through me, and I only felt a slight twinge of pain when he inserted his finger. But I was so wet for him, that it went away as fast as it came.

"Cum for me, Victoria." He demanded between licks, and my body complied with his wish. My head was further back, and my arms could barely hold my upper body up, crying out his name over and over as my body convulsed. When the tremors subsided, he slowly brought me back down.

He looked at me, "I never thought I would have such an affection for these countertops," chuckling, he pulled his shirt back down to cover me up, and helped me put my panties back on. Lifting me down, I nearly fell my legs were so weeks. "Finally, you can't walk." Laughing, he held me still for a few moments.

When I was able to let go, I got a cloth and cleaned off the counter, and started to make breakfast. But I had plans for him later, *'Two can play this game, Mr. Lycan.'* I thought to myself.

Grayson had been given a couple of days away from his duties. And we spent those getting to know one another. When I realized what day it was, I asked him for my laptop. "Does Levi still have my laptop?"

Grayson was chopping some vegetables, shaking his head no. "I put it down in my corridor with your notebooks for safe-keeping."

"What corridor?" asking confused, as I snatched a carrot and popped it in my mouth.

Pulling me close, "Down in the tunnels." He explained, "We each have one." Then he asked. "Why do you need it?"

Sighing, "Grayson, I need to pay my rent. And I need to decide what I am going to do about my thesis." I didn't move from his arms, I loved being close to him.

Grayson didn't try to take over the issue. "What do you want to do about your thesis?"

Shrugging, "I don't know." There was a hint of defeat in my voice, "I am not even sure what I can do. Professor Maxwell was my advisor, and for obvious reasons, I can't very well tell Stamford University where he is."

As we sat and ate that a thought came to my mind. "I should probably send an email to Tavish, his assistant. And talk to him."

"Who did you say?" Grayson's eyes were intent, and I could tell my answer was going to be important.

"Tavish," replying with a shrug, "I don't know his last name. But he has been with the professor for a couple of years now."

"Would you recognize him? In a picture?" Grayson was acting strange, and I could tell he was agitated.

"Sure," I said, then he took my hand, and we left our house.

He took my hand, and we walked over to Levi's he pounded on the door. When Levi answered, "I need a picture of Tavish." He insisted. Levi nodded and walked into his house. When he came back, he held out a couple of papers to me.

Looking at them I saw my professor's assistant, but he had changed his appearance slightly in each photograph. "That's him. Why do you have pictures of the professor's assistant?"

Neither Grayson nor Levi answered me, they both just growled low. Grayson took my hand and led me home. "Stay in the house, Victoria." Then he took me to the door I thought led to the basement. "At any sign of trouble, you come here." Then he pushed in a code, 1290, the door opened, when I looked in there were stairs leading down. "There is a flashlight here, but you should be able to see in the dark. Take the stairs down into the tunnels. You will be safe down there." He was worried, and I was confused about what was happening. But I paid attention to what he was telling me, nodding that I understood.

Over the next few days, Grayson was gone most of the time. Only coming home to shower, and strip to go to bed. Only once did he ask me to write down the name of my apartment manager and email, without telling me why.

My emotions were all over the place, mostly I was frightened for Grayson and the others. So much so that I noticed some changes happening to me that scared me. Grayson was busy, and I didn't want to bother him, I became distant. Staying quiet most of the time, not even talking to Samantha. I had to think.

Chapter 21

Grayson

Victoria was in more danger than before. She knew Tavish and that scared the shit out of me. Tavish was smart, and a master of disguising himself, and he knew who and what we are, and that made him extremely dangerous. Levi still has not been able to find out much about him through his extensive search.

We upped our security around the compound, and I was more protective of Victoria, and would not let her out of the house, checking and re-checking on her constantly. There was a tightening in my chest of the fear of losing her. But something more was bothering her; it was not just the fear she sensed in me. But every time I asked, she would just say she was fine. So, I didn't press her.

Lucas was much in the same way with Samantha and their young, threatening to send her to Scotland to her father's. She had just had a new infant daughter and was hardly out of their bedroom since she was taking care of her. One afternoon he offered to send Victoria with them if it came to that point, but Samantha was adamant that she would not leave her home, and that the baby was too young to travel such a long distance.

But he said if he had to fling her over his shoulder to get her on the plane he would.

Now over a week has passed, and still nothing. We were all stalking around like wild animals. The wait for something to happen was torture. Levi with Patrick, and two of his men, went to California. They asked around the university but found out that Tavish had disappeared around the same time as the professor. Slipping out of our grasp again.

But I had Levi go on two additional missions as well. He hired a moving company to pack up Victoria's apartment and ship her belonging here, as well as pay off her lease. Then I had him station two guards to watch after her father. If anything happened to him, Victoria would never forgive me. A part of me felt bad going against her wishes of fixing her problems for her, but I was just too occupied with keeping her safe.

Levi and Patrick came back somewhat defeated that Tavish was back in the wind. Lucas was on the phone and video calls with the high council nearly daily keeping them informed of what was going on, and since he didn't have anything to report the high council was getting frustrated at our lack of progress. But there was nothing we could do but wait.

It was early morning, and I was in the kitchen, last night I could not stay away from Victoria, I needed her near me and I needed to have her. We mated most of the night, and I left her sound asleep in our bed.

She came down sleepy and beautiful, wearing one of my t-shirts. She just walked up to me and wrapped her arms around me coming up on her tiptoes to kiss me. I picked her up, and instinctively she wrapped her legs around me, and I deepened the kiss. I felt it the second she bit me, pulling back she saw the blood on my lip. "Oh my god!" shocked, she covered her mouth to find her teeth had grown into fangs. Pushing against me, she asked, "How?" When she pushed against me again, I set her feet back on the floor.

Before she could run back upstairs, I rested my hands on her shoulders, "Victoria, I am fine. Look."

Turning, tears stung her eyes, but even through them, she could see that I was no longer bleeding. "What's happening to me?" she whispered.

When I tried to bring Victoria back into my arms, she pulled away, "I can't," shaking her head, "I hurt you," I could hear the anguish in her voice.

Unfortunately, a knock came at the front door, and as I went to answer it, she walked back upstairs. I knew she was scared, and I fully intended to talk to her, but the day got away from me, and by the time I got back home, she had moved her things into the guest bedroom. When I knew she was asleep, I crawled into bed with her.

Chapter 22

Victoria

The changes started when I woke up from when I had been shot, but at first, they were so gradual, being able to see in the dark and hearing and smelling things in a distance, seemed fun. But now the changes were happening faster and faster. My nails would grow, if I was worried, or one morning I nicked myself shaving in the shower, getting out I saw my teeth had grown and looked like fangs. I stayed in the bathroom until they were normal. And when I bit him yesterday morning, it was the last straw for me, I had to stay away from him. When I went upstairs, I moved my meager belongings into the guest room, but Grayson didn't stay away from me. He had known something was bothering me, but every time he asked I would just say I was fine, but the truth is I was far from fine.

Even Samantha noticed that I was being distant. I thought about talking to her. But she had little Aileen to take care of, I just could not bring myself to burden her. As far as I knew a human had not been changed into a Lycan in thousands of years. So that left me with no one I could talk to about what was happening to me. I felt so alone.

Grayson was in the training fields working with the recruits, and Lucas was staying close to home, taking care of Samantha as she took care of their little ones. I didn't know where the others were, somewhere in the compound I assumed. The walls of our home were closing in, and I needed to get out just to take a walk and think. Stopping and looked at the entrance of the mines, I had never been down there I knew that is where they had imprisoned the professor. Grayson told me that there were several levels to the mine, and the professor was in one of the deepest ones where they had cells. And he told me my research notebooks and laptop were in his corridor.

Just as I was about to continue a figure slipping into the entrance caught my attention, I could not see his face, and I just thought it was one of the recruits that I had not met. Honestly, I didn't know most of them, but there was just something about this one that was vaguely familiar.

Transfixed on the entrance I stood still, as soon as the alarm went off, the hairs on the back of my neck tingled. There was trouble, my feet were frozen in place when the one whom I assumed was the recruit and the professor came running out. That is when I recognized him, it was Tavish! Just then the professor pointed and yelled at me, "Grab her, she knows where it is!"

Terror welled up inside of me, when I looked down at my hands, as my fingernails turned into claws, and extended from my hands. My body shook and contorted, nearly painfully. Tavish came running toward me he held a gun in his hand, turning when Levi came running out of his house growling. He turned and brought the gun around pointing at Levi, screaming, "You! I will have my vengeance on you! I will kill you as your grandfather killed mine." Before he could shoot, I slashed at him with my claws, ripping through his shirt, he screamed in pain as blood flowed from his back, dropping the gun. Turning he looked at me, "You are one of them! Beast!" Then he ran past me to get away.

Out of the corner of my eye, I saw the professor run forward to get to the gun, I watched as he grabbed it, swung it around he pointed it at me. "Victoria!" I heard Grayson yell. He was running toward me, his Lycan was coming out with each step he took. The professor turned the gun and aimed it at Grayson.

"MINE!" something screamed in my head, then acting on instinct, to protect my mate. I reached out and with strength, I didn't know I possessed, my clawed hand encompassed his throat, squeezing and lifting him off the ground, the professor dropped the gun and floundered around like a fish on a hook. When he went limp, I dropped him on the ground, looking down at what I had done, then up at Grayson, now back in his human form. Levi was standing still, not far behind, looking at me. I could have reached out and touched Grayson, he was slowly walking toward me. "Victoria?" He whispered, "It is okay. Don't be afraid." But I was afraid, shaking my head, I backed away, turned, and ran back into our home. My reflection in the mirror that was just in the foray stopped me. There I saw what the man had said. *I am a beast!*

Howling in terror I could not stand to see what I had become. I ran out of the back of the house to the forest. Only stopping when I came to the lake where we mated by our first night together. My world was perfect then. But now, I know I am a beast, and probably just killed the professor. How could Grayson love me now? Sinking to my knees I wept until I had no more tears left.

As my tears were spent, I felt myself change back to my human form, I watched with fascination as my hands returned to normal. Too afraid to return to the house, would Grayson despise me now, seeing that I killed? I continued to sit looking out to the lake, as the sun started to set in the west.

Grayson finally came looking for me, I knew he could find me. There was no place on this earth I could hide from him. He had my scent, and I had his. I didn't turn or acknowledge him when he sat beside me lifting me onto his lap.

He tried to bring my face up to look at him, but I was too afraid to see the disgust in his eyes. Pushing his hand away, he let go, but pulled me closer to his chest and held me there. The rhythmic beating of his heart calmed me. "Will I go to prison?" I whispered.

Not letting go, he asked, "Why would you go to prison?"

It was hard to say the words, but I knew in my heart, that I had committed the ultimate sin. "Because I killed the professor." I turned my head into his chest and tears I didn't think I had any more of came.

Grayson let me cry, rubbing his hand up and down my back. He knew I would not listen until I had calmed. When I stopped, Grayson said, "Victoria, the professor is not dead."

"But I.." I could not say the words.

"Victoria, look at me please." I could hear the worry in his voice. Slowly I did as he asked and sat up to look into his eyes. He reached up with his hands and held my face still, "You did not kill him." Letting that information sink in, he continued. "The professor will have some trouble talking for a few weeks. His throat is swollen and bruised, but he is alive."

Nodding, "But I wanted to kill him." Uttering my confession, "He was going to kill you. I could not let him."

Grayson leaned closer to my face and kissed my nose. "The gun he had only held tranquilizing darts. He would not have killed me."

Confused, "Darts? I don't understand." I started to shiver from a deep chill, "But I thought. I could have killed him." I felt like a murderer, and I was in my heart. I wanted the professor dead for what he has done. To me, Grayson, and my father, I have never felt such hatred for anyone before, and this scared me. I pushed against Grayson, and he let me up.

Standing he reached out and took my hands, "Come let's get you home and in a hot bathtub, you are shivering, and you don't have your kilt." He didn't understand, and I could not tell him, there was a war going on in my head. So, I followed along, and let him get me in the tub, and then to bed. Exhaustion won out and I fell asleep.

Chapter 23

Grayson

As soon as the alarms when off we all ran from the training fields, my first instinct was to get to Victoria. My Lycan emerged to protect her, but as I came into the courtyard, I saw Victoria in her Lycan form. I could feel her terror about what was happening to her. I watched as she slashed at Tavish's back when he tried to shoot Levi. Then she protected me, from being shot by the professor. Quickly, I came back to my human side, and slowly stepped toward her I only wanted to comfort her, but she ran. Just a few seconds after she entered our house, I heard the anguish in her howl. My first instinct was to go run her, but I had to help clean up this mess.

Looking down, the professor was moving and having trouble breathing. I knelt to see the damage done to his throat from Victoria when I saw Lucas coming forward, "We need Dr. Herbert." I called out. Lucas nodded and turned on his heel going back into his house.

Levi came beside me and lifted the professor muttering, "I would just like to let him die." The professors' eyes widened with fear at his words, but he could not speak, thankfully. Levi carried him to his house. Coming back out he asked, "Did you hear what Tavish yelled at me?" At my nod, he continued, "I think I may know who this Tavish is. But I need to do some digging, and my grandmother's diary is down in the tunnels, it may shed some light as well."

Nodding that I had heard him, "I need to go down to find out what happened to the guards." My mind was on Victoria, and the sooner we got this mess cleaned up the sooner I could go to her, turning I headed for the tunnels but looked in the direction of the lake. I just hoped she stopped there; it has a special meaning to both of us.

Wyatt was already down, helping one of the guards to the elevator, I grabbed another and hefted him over my shoulder, and followed along. "He used darts," Wyatt said and handed me one that he had pulled out of the guard. Noah had the third guard, and we all headed up to the ground level, laying them out for Jackson to take over their care.

Lucas came out of his house, "The Doctor is on her way." He announced. He picked up the gun and walked to me. "Grayson a word." He motioned away from the others. "Has she changed before today?"

Lowering my head, "Yes and no, we were kissing the other morning and her fangs came out and she bit me, but as far as her Lycan coming fully to the surface not that I know of." Then I looked out to the woods, "I think she has had some changes happening since we mated. But she has been distant and would not tell me."

Lucas was my friend and commander, "Like a baby Lycan, her fear took over and her Lycan came out." Patting me on the back, "Go find her. We can take care of things here." As I turned to leave, "Grayson, whatever she needs, we are here to help." Lucas called out.

Not sure of what she needed, I was born a Lycan, but I turned her. She had to hate me for what was happening. Slowly I walked out to the woods, following her scent. Right where I thought she would be, she was sitting looking out to the lake. Still, with no idea how to help her, I stood back and watched as she wiped tears from her face, then she watched her hands as her claws retreated.

She didn't acknowledge me when I sat beside her, but I put her on my lap anyway. Victoria pushed my hand away when I tried to get her to look at me. What she didn't understand was that I would never let her go no matter how hard she tried to push me away. That was the message I was trying to get across when she moved into the guest room. So, I just tightened my hold, hopefully getting the point across. When she finally asked if she would be going to prison, I sighed. Thankfully she was talking. I spent the next few minutes convincing her that the professor was alive. But that knowledge didn't seem to help much.

Finally, when she pushed at me again, I let her up, taking her hand. We went back home. She was silent as we walked and stayed silent as I ran her a bath and undressed her. Once I finally got her into bed and she fell asleep. I quietly slipped out of the house and went to Lucas'.

He opened the door, and Samantha walked up to me, hugging me. "How is she?" she asked.

Returning the hug, "Quiet. Too quiet." I muttered.

"Samantha, go to bed," Lucas ordered. "You are tired." She turned to say something, but Lucas just growled low and deep. I had to turn my head to hide a smile. "Grayson." He motioned for me to follow him into his office. "What's going on?"

Nearly falling into a chair, "I don't know what to do for her." Confessing my fear. "I did this to her, Lucas. I am responsible for turning her into a Lycan, it was my blood."

Lucas is always levelheaded. "Do you regret saving her life?"

"No!" My answer was adamant.

Nodding, "Then let's move on." Thinking. "Did she say anything to you?"

A small smile came to my lips, "Only she was afraid of going to prison for killing the professor." Sighing, "It took me some time to convince her that he was still alive. Not that I care, how is he?"

"He will live. Dr. Herbert said he would not be talking until the swelling went down." Smiling, "I made a couple of calls, he will not be our problem for long." Raising his hand, "We will talk about that later."

Coming back to our original topic, "What do I do for her, Lucas?"

Looking up, "I have an idea. But it isn't like I have a way to contact him."

Confused, "Who?"

A small smile played across Lucas' face, "We only know of one that could tell her about what is happening to her. The one that created the first Lycan."

"Eryn?" I asked incredulously. Lucas nodded. "But how do we get ahold of him?" I wondered out loud.

Lucas said, "We know he goes to see the treasure from time to time." Then sighing, "I just hope he is watching and knows of Victoria's situation."

I sighed, "I better get back to her," standing. I walked to the front door, "I hope you are right and he shows, Lucas." I said and quietly shut the door.

Thankfully Victoria was still asleep when I got home, not being able to sleep just yet, I walked downstairs to find Eryn standing out on my back porch.

"Grayson," he said and motioned for me to come forward. "I am here to help her." That was all he said, then he stepped down the stairs before I could offer him the guest room. "I will stay in the cave." As he walked away, three guards followed him along.

The next morning, I awoke to find Victoria gone, I knew where she was. Eryn was back on my porch, "She left about twenty minutes ago." We walked to the lake in silence until we reached Victoria.

Chapter 24

Victoria

It is early morning the sun was just now coming up. I had not slept all last night. Not wanting to wake Grayson or have him worry about me, I slipped out of our bed and came out to the lake. Staring out across the water, I was calm, but still very afraid of what I had become last night. Grayson said that he didn't know if I would change into a Lycan when he gave me his blood. And it didn't happen right away. But last night I did, and it scared the shit out of me.

As I sit here by the pond, I needed to think. But I could not possibly put into words what I feel. Tears streamed down my face; *Can Grayson still desire me?* I wondered. Not usually a conceited person, even I saw my reflection in the mirror of what I had become.

The snap of a twig alerted me to someone approaching. "Grayson, I just need to think," I called out.

Stepping closer, it was not only Grayson that came into my site. "Victoria, this is Lord Eryn a friend." A man dressed in a red suit came into my view, his eyes were kind, and his hair was as white as snow. He bowed his head as Grayson introduced him.

My eyes darted to Grayson then back to the stranger, "Sir." I bowed my head to him.

Grayson offered me his hand so that I could stand, "Victoria, Lord Eryn, would like to speak with you about what happened last night."

"A therapist? Really?" I whispered harshly.

"I am not a therapist, Victoria." The stranger offered with a grin. Then he came close to me and presented me with his arm, then said. "Now first call me Eryn." Then patting my hand, "Shall we take a stroll?' Then he turned his eyes up to Grayson, "You come to, Grayson. So that Victoria is comfortable."

"My Lord," Grayson bowed his head and stepped back with his hands behind his back, allowing Lord Eryn and I to pass. It was strange, I had never seen Grayson act with such reverence to anyone, not even to Lucas. Who I now know is his commander.

Eryn led me through the trees, "I understand your Lycan came to the surface last night." I nodded and glanced back to Grayson, he smiled and winked at me to reassure me he was there. The stranger patted my hand that was placed in his arm, "I am not here to harm you, Victoria. And Grayson is right there to protect you if needed."

Sighing, I answered, "Yes sir, and it scared the ..." I stopped speaking before I cursed in front of him. He is older than me and my manners took over.

There was a chuckle from him. "No need to hold back your words, Victoria. I have heard them all." Then he continued, "Now tell me this, when Grayson's Lycan emerges are you afraid?"

"No," I answered honestly.

"But your Lycan does," it was not a question but a statement.

"Yes," I whispered lowering my head in shame. "Grayson saved my life by giving me his blood, and I am grateful to be alive. But I feel like I should be proud like him and the others to be a Lycan, but I am afraid." Grayson stepped closer to comfort me, but the stranger waved him back.

He turned and faced me. "Victoria," his voice was calm, and gently he raised my face to look at him. "If you had a choice, would you prefer not to be a Lycan?"

Confused, "You mean to die?"

Eryn shook his head, "No not at all, but if you could go back to being a human with only a small amount of Grayson's blood as things have been done for centuries." Before I could answer, "You will live a long time, but no longer will your Lycan come forth, and your ability to heal, see and hear will be gone." He was looking at me with intent, "Be sure before you answer."

Not sure of how to answer, "I don't know. Would that mean my Lycan half would die?"

He didn't seem offended by my answer, and answered me honestly, "Yes, in a way."

My eyes widened and a tear escaped, "I don't think I want to let that part of me die." Then after a moment, I nodded, "I am sure I don't want that part of me to die." Looking at Eryn, in the eyes, I was sure.

"Good, now I want you to do me a favor." He patted my hand.

Nodding, "Okay," I said. My eyes didn't leave his face, I was still too ashamed to glance at Grayson for fear of seeing the disappointment on his face at my confession of being afraid.

The stranger spoke again, "Close your eyes, and concentrate on your beast within."

Confused, "I don't understand," I said.

His eyes didn't leave my face, "Your beast, and you are one, and separate too. Close your eyes and communicate with your beast."

Slowly I closed my eyes, even though I felt silly. After a moment I heard a voice, it was like my own but deeper. Similar to what I heard in my head, as the Professor pointed the gun at Grayson. I let go of Lord Eryn and raised my hand to rub over my heart. A tear slipped from my eye again as my beast spoke to me. Opening my eyes, "She is afraid too." I whispered.

The stranger, nodded, "You are the first human in more than a millennium to be transformed into a Lycan." Taking my arm back into his, "Lycaon was afraid when he was transformed as were all the humans that he changed. Including the Princes' who your mate is descendent from."

When I looked confused, "Princes?"

The stranger looked at Grayson as he spoke to me, "Your education in Lycan history has been lacking some I see." Since he was smiling, I assumed he was not angry.

Grayson spoke for the first time. "It will be remedied, My Lord." He lowered his eyes.

The Eryn just bowed his head, "See that it is." Though his tone was not angry, it sounded like a command.

Lord Eryn smiled but glanced at Grayson, "Grayson and the others will have to take care and teach you how to control your beast within. Like a young Lycan pup, you need to learn to control your beast, right now she is appearing when your emotions are out of control."

Then he turned toward us a path toward a cave, "Now I would like to introduce Victoria to my daughter." He looked me in the eye deeply, "I assume you can keep a secret, my dear?"

"Yes," I answered. Not sure what was going to happen, but something told me it was going to be of some significance.

We walked into a darkened cave when Eryn raised his hand, and torches along the walls lit showing us a path. As we walked deeper and deeper into the cave the torches ahead of us lit as the ones behind extinguished their flames. Then we came to a large cavern. The Eryn stopped patting my hand. I let go and watched as he stepped forward to a golden sarcophagus. He then placed his hand on the carved hands of a woman and bowed his head.

Stepping back, I bumped into Grayson, he put his hands on my shoulders and bowed his head as well. Not sure what to do, I folded my hands in front of me and bowed my head as well. It was a few minutes when the stranger came in front of me again. "Victoria, your journey that led you to find Grayson started with a treasure hunt." Gesturing towards the sarcophagus, "This is my daughter Mary. And I will not have humans dissecting her and studying her remains." Patting my hand, he motioned again to a bench, "Come let us sit."

Following him, to a bench. I sat beside him. When he told me a story. "A very long time ago after I transformed Lycaon into the first Lycan. Humans started turning away from the gods they had once prayed to." He paused and looked over to the sarcophagus, clasping my hand in his, as he spoke, I could see the images in my mind. "I decided to live as a human and suppressed my powers."

Nodding that I understood, though I was not sure I did, he continued. "I fell in love and took a human to be my wife. After a time, she bore me a human daughter, Mary." He turned his head and love in his eyes was evident as he gazed at her again. "When she came of age, Mary chose to follow the one the humans were referring to as their savior. She even married him, but after he was crucified, I thought she would come home, but she didn't. Refusing to interfere in her life, I returned to Olympus, there were pressing matters that needed my attention, but I continued to watch after her." There was now a sadness in his eyes, "She traveled so far and ended up in Ephesus, where she died. The humans buried her, but I had this made and hid her remains, but not well enough. She was found."

A flash of anger crossed his face, "The Templars kept her safe for a time, but I knew that with the end of the crusades, the Pope would seize her as their own or destroy her. And I could not allow that to happen, so I had Guillaume de Beaujeu entrust her remains with Grayson's and the other's grandfathers to keep her safe and away from humans for all time." When he finished speaking, he waved his hand again, and more torches lit in the cavern showing six knights standing in a circle guarding the sarcophagus.

Standing and walking up to one, "Are they dead?" I asked.

"No, just suspended in time," Eryn said.

Walking around each, I came to the one that Grayson looked so much alike, "Is this your grandfather?" I asked him.

He smiled, "He is." Grayson stepped beside me and introduced me, "Victoria, this is my grandfather, Gavin Sinclair."

Gently I placed my hand on his breastplate, and I whispered. "I am so happy to meet you." A thick Scottish deep voice sounded in my head. *'Aye, Lass. And I am happy to meet you, Victoria. You will be a fine mate for my grandson."* I looked over my shoulder to Grayson, "Did he just speak to me?"

Grayson nodded, "Yes." Then he turned me so we could give our full attention back to Eryn. "Lord Eryn, my apologies."

Leading me back I sat beside the man again, "Victoria. My name is not Eryn, though your mate and his friends refer to me as such." He paused, looking me in the eye, instead of telling me who he is, he asked me a question. "Victoria, what do you know of what humans call Greek Mythology?"

Confused as to where his question is leading, "That Zeus, was the king of the gods, and the god of the sky also the most powerful. Hades and Poseidon were his brothers. And there were twelve Olympian gods altogether that were the main deities."

Eryn nodded as I spoke, "Now, I am going to tell you a secret, that even the high council does not know." He paused then said, "I am Zeus." As he said his name, he changed. Now in a white robe belted at his waist, and his hair was dark, a crown of golden olive leaves circled his head.

Completely in shock, I looked over to Grayson, his head was bowed. Then I noticed that all six of the knights had bowed their heads too. *This couldn't be, it had to be a trick. Maybe I was dreaming.* I looked back to Zeus/Eryn, and he had changed back to the way he first presented himself to me. He patted my arm, "You are not dreaming, my dear. This form suits me and is more comforting to most. So, I continue to present myself as Eryn."

He stood and walked past the sarcophagus, and waved his hand, following behind him, now torches all around were fully ablaze, and I could see that this cavern went on and that there was more than just the sarcophagus in this cavern. "I have had these items hidden from humans as well, they are dangerous in their hands, and must never be found." He turned and the torches went out. Sighing, he said, "I would like to spend some time with my daughter alone. Grayson, please take Victoria home, she needs to rest."

Grayson nodded, and stepped forward, "Come Victoria." Taking my hand, we walked out of the cave; the torches lit our path. Neither of us said a word until we were back at the lake. Leading me to a tree, he sat down bringing me with him, then placed me on his lap.

"What just happened?" I asked, laying my head on his shoulder.

"Lord Eryn showed you the treasure that was entrusted to our grandfathers." He said, "As well as the other objects we are sworn to protect."

Sitting up, and looking into his eyes, "I am sorry."

Grayson smiled, feeling the tension in me, and he started to rub my back. "What are you sorry for?"

He caught my head as I tried to look away and down to my hands, I had no choice but to continue to look him in the eye. "For being afraid, and not being proud like you to be a Lycan." A tear ran down my cheek.

Leaning forward he kissed my tear away. "Victoria, you have no reason to be ashamed of your fear. And you do not need to apologize to me or anyone because of it." Sighing seeing that his words were not making me feel better. "I was born a Lycan, and have had more than four hundred years of learning to control my beast and my powers around humans."

I nodded but still didn't feel much better. He continued, as he took my hand with his and extended it out in front of us both, "With me, let your claws extend." My hand was flat on his, and his claws started to extend from his fingers, but mine didn't.

"I guess I am broken." I chuckled nervously.

Grayson was not going to let me give up, "Close your eyes, and communicate with your beast, work together." I did as he said and closed my eyes, "Breath, Victoria. Deep breathes." As I relaxed, my nails extended. "Good, very good."

Opening my eyes, I looked down to see that my claws were extended. "I did it." Whispering.

Grayson nodded, "Now, bring them back in." Not closing my eyes again, I took a calming breath, and as Grayson's claws retreated into his hand so did mine.

Grayson hugged me tight, "Most young Lycans cannot control their beasts, when they become upset their beast can emerge. It takes time for them to learn to control them." I could feel him smiling, "Your Lycan is as old as you, but still a baby at the same time." Then he moved me so I could look him in the eye, "You were afraid last night, that is why your Lycan came out, she was protecting you."

"So, I need to learn to control my Lycan." Even though I repeated what Grayson had just said, I need to say it for myself to understand. "But can you still desire me, even with the way I looked last night?"

Holding me close, "Let me ask you a question to answer yours. When we mated for the first time, and my Lycan emerged, did you still desire me?"

"Of course!" I sat up and looked into his eyes. Then I smiled, leaning close, "Grayson, I need you." Whispering my mouth was just a breath away from his. Letting the tip of my tongue slide out I traced his lips.

Grayson inhaled, as his fingers came around my head, pulling my mouth to his, growling, "Then you shall have me." His kiss was not gentle by any means, and I loved the feel of his possessiveness. Again, we stayed out by the lake until the pink streaks of the morning were coming up in the east.

Chapter 25

Grayson

It has been several days since Lord Eryn came and visited with Victoria. She has been taking time each day to concentrate on controlling her beast. I have found her several times out at the lake meditating. She said that communicating with her beast was easier out here with the calm of the water. So, I didn't interfere.

Noah and Levi left with the professor early this morning, escorting him to Scotland. The high council finally agreed with Lucas that it was too dangerous to keep him here. There is a Lycan prison in the highlands, where he would be kept for the rest of his days. I still wanted to tear him limb from limb, for hurting Victoria.

Walking to our home, I had forgotten about her things arriving today, until I got the call just a little while ago. Now I had to explain to her that I mettled. When I entered our home, she was sitting out on the back porch. "Grayson," she called out with a smile as I walked up. Her legs were drawn up to her chest, and a cup of coffee was between her hands.

I leaned against the railing and looked at her, "Victoria, I did something you may not be happy with." I stated.

She tilted her head to the side, "Did you kill the professor?" she smiled at the thought.

"No, I did not." I chuckled at her blood lust. "When Levi went to California to search for Tavish. I had him hire movers to pack up your apartment and then shipped everything here." My arms were crossed over my chest, and I was waiting for her to get mad.

"I know." She said, at my confused look. She explained. "My landlord called and told me. And she said that you also paid off my rental agreement."

"You are not angry?" I asked.

She shook her head, "No, with everything that has been going on, it is just one less thing I have to worry about. Thank you."

Nodding, I pushed away from the railing, she reached out and clasped my hand, "And thank you for protecting my father."

"You know about that too?" asking, I had not intended on telling her, because I didn't want her to worry.

Another smile, "Yes, he called me and said that one of the guards you have watching him, escorted him home." Then she laughed, "He has them now living at his apartment. Said that it was easier that way." She shrugged. Standing she asked, "Will we see Lord Eryn again?"

Pushing away from the railing, I followed her into the house, "I don't know. He shows up when he wants to, and not very often. He came to see you as a favor to me." She walked into the kitchen washed her cup then put it away. "Did you need to talk to him about something?" I asked.

Victoria smiled, and I could see that she was coming to terms with being a Lycan, "No, I just wanted to show him that I am learning to control my Lycan." Shrugging, "That's all."

Wrapping my arms around her waist, "How about we go for a ride on my bike, and you can show me? I know of a nice, secluded spot on the opposite side of the lake." Whispering into her ear. "And if you want you can let your Lycan out to mate with mine."

Her eyes became dilated with excitement, then she frowned. "Can you take time away from your duties?"

My eyes flashed, as I growled low, "To spend time with you? Yes." Taking her hand, we walked out the front door, just as the moving truck pulled up. I could sense the disappointment when she let go of my hand. Before she move away from me, I whistled and motioned for a couple of the recruits to come forward. Leaning down I whispered, "What use are they if I can't get them to do some menial labor for me?" She turned her head and giggled.

After I ordered them to unload the truck, and where to put her belongings. I went to the barn and grabbed one of my bikes. She smiled and asked, as I offered her a hand to climb behind me, "Is this new?"

Chuckling, "No, I have several." She wrapped her hands around my waist and laid her head on my back. I took some back roads around the property, and we stopped at the top of a hill that looked over a large expanse of the property, getting off she walked around looking at everything. "Grayson, this is beautiful."

Leaning on my bike I watched her with new eyes for what was around me. "This is one of my favorite places on the property. I come up here when I needed to be alone, or worried about finding you."

She turned at my statement, "Why were you worried about finding me?"

Glancing down to my hands then back to her eyes, "A Lycan can go mad if they do not find their mate. It has been known to happen."

She stepped toward me, and I spread my legs so that she could be as close as possible. Laying her hands on my chest, my beast nudged her. "Well, I guess you don't have to worry about that any longer."

Leaning down I kissed her softly, "No I guess not." Then I offered my hand to get back on the bike, "We have a date by the lake." Again she climbed on behind me, and bringing her arms around my waist, she stroked my chest as I drove through the back down the road toward the opposite side of the lake. Once I put the kickstand in place and got off, I lifted her down to the ground. Then leaned again on my bike, as I watched her walk around exploring.

The sun was about to set, and as she walked up in between my legs, she smiled as her hands trailed down my abdomen, then to the fly of my jeans, "Grayson? Can I?"

A low growl came from me, "You can do anything you want to me, Victoria. I am yours alone."

She slowly rubbed the bulge in my pants and licked her lips. "Anything?"

Another growl came from deep inside of me, "Anything." I confirmed, her eyes flashed yellow as she slowly released my belt, then unbuttoned my jeans. Tentatively one of her hands slide into my jeans as the other unzipped my fly.

When she went down to her knees and pulled my cock free from my jeans, I watched as her tongue darted out to lick the tip of my head. Precum was already seeping out, "Oh yum, Grayson," she whispered before opening her mouth wide and taking me inside.

My head went back at the exquisite feel of her hot mouth around my cock, and I growled low with pleasure. Threading my fingers through her hair, I guided her back and forth, "Can you take more?" I asked as I pushed further into her throat. One hand was on my thigh, and the other was stroking my shaft as she sucked back and forth, allowing her saliva to coat me. Soon an orgasm was building, my balls tightened, and growling, "I am going to cum, Victoria!" With my cock in her mouth, she nodded that she was ready. Throwing back my head I howled as my semen jetted out hitting the back of her throat, she sucked and swallowed what I gave her.

She smiled up at me as she licked the last drop from her lip, I reached down and helped her up then turned her to face my bike. Moving close to her, I nuzzled her and I licked her, while one hand fondled her breast up under her shirt, and with my other I worked at getting her pants open, Slipping my hand down through her panties, playing with her clit, I slipped a finger into her core, "You are wet for me, Victoria," Her answer to moan. I knew I could bring her to orgasm with my hand, but I wanted to taste her, so I withdrew my hand. Quickly I pushed her pants down and stripped her of them with her shoes. Then spreading her legs I pulled them back, "Lean over the seat of my bike." I ordered.

She did as she was told, and when I spread her buttocks wide, I ran my nose over her, "Your nectar is just too sweet for me to resist." She moaned again, I rewarded her with the tip of my tongue flicking over her clit, then moving back to slip into her core.

"Grayson," she moaned again, her legs trembled but stayed where she was, as I feasted on her. Slipping a finger up into her, I fucked her slow at first, then as her cries of pleasure came harder, I added another and quickened my pace.

Her body shook harder, and I knew she was about to cum as well as having a hard time controlling her beast as well. "Cum for me, Victoria," I said then she exploded all over my face. Licking up her nectar as it flowed as I continued to fuck her with my fingers, her body convulsed around them. As she quieted, I stood, kicking off my boots and then my jeans, my cock was rock hard. I covered her from behind, threading my fingers with hers. "Together, Victoria," I said into her ear.

She knew exactly what I meant, as I slowly slipped my cock up into her, she took a deep breath, and started to contort with me. Our beasts mated together until we both came again, then I returned to my human side, coming out of her, I whispered to her until she too was back. When she was back to her human side, I turned her to face me and sat her up on my bike seat.

I held onto her ass as I thrust deep into her again, one of her hands gripped the front tip of the seat, and she raised her leg to wrap around my waist so I could go deeper as I thrust. Her other hand was around my neck, as she looked down at our joined bodies.

She looked up into my eyes, as hers flashed yellow, growling, "More!" she cried out her demand, and I was more than happy to comply. Her head went back exposing her neck, and I let my fangs out to scrap over the sensitive skin. "Grayson!" She cried again, and her body tightened. I thrust hard three times, and she let go without me telling her. As her core convulsed around my cock, I let go and filled her with my semen again.

She went limp against me and I lifted her down to the ground. Leaning her against the bike I slipped my shirt up over my head and tossed it with the rest of our clothes. Picking her up, Victoria immediately wrapped her legs around me as I carried her into the water of the lake. She shrieked when I lowered her down into the cool water, but she let me wash her off, then ran to grab my shirt. I came out a moment later, slipping on my jeans as I lead her to a soft spot on the grass and laid down with her. Snuggling close, "Grayson?"

Kissing the top of her head, "Yes."

"I like this bike. How many did you say you have?" she asked.

Hearing the smile in her voice, I answered. "The one I had in Scotland, these one and two others. Why?"

She was rubbing my chest and abdomen, "I think we are going to have to try out the others before I can choose which one, I like the best." She giggled.

Rubbing her back I laughed, "We can do that, and I will buy more so we can test those as well if you want."

She didn't answer, I heard her breathing start to even out. I let her sleep, then woke her up before dawn to mate again, before I took her home.

Chapter 26

Victoria

These last few months have been one change after another. But I would not change my life now for the world. As Grayson promised, we tried out his other bikes at the lake, but I always would say I wasn't sure, we needed to test one or the other again before I could make a decision. He caught on to what I was doing and laughed.

I had unpacked my belongings and mingled them throughout the house, at first, I was unsure about what he would think. He just caressed my check, "This is your home, Victoria. Do as you like."

One night, we sat out on the porch, and he told me about the official mating ceremony. "It is like what humans call a wedding." He explained.

Looking over to him, shocked, "Grayson those take months and months to plan." I argued.

In his fashion, "You have a week and a half." He shrugged.

Now I not only had a ceremony to plan, but it was nearing my time to present my thesis, and I was not sure what I was going to do. I walked over to see Samantha to get her advice on our mating ceremony. She had little Aileen in her arms, and I looked longing at the sweet baby.

Seeing my reaction, "As much time as you two spend out at the lake, you will have one soon." She teased.

Blushing, that she knew all along what we were doing we discussed my mating ceremony, "Who do I invite?" I started.

She thought for a moment as the baby fell asleep, then she walked into the living room placing her gently into a bassinet. When she came back into the kitchen. She sat, as I stood and started some tea. Samantha was taking care of two babies, and now helping me, I could at least make her a cup of tea.

Smiling, "Murdoc of course," at the look of confusion on my face, "Grayson's brother." She explained.

Then she listed off several others, Liam, Lucas's brother, and several members of the high council. I added. "Your father."

"My father?" she asked.

I smiled, "He said when we were there, that he expected an invitation."

Nodding, "He is coming tomorrow to see the baby, anyway. I am sure he would love to stay." Then she looked concerned, "You have not mentioned your father."

Looking out to the woods through the French doors, "I am not sure how to explain, everything..." I waved my hand over myself.

"That is a dilemma." Looking up at the front door opening, she smiled and put her finger to her lips. Then said in a clear voice, "I will have to ask Lucas to take me for a ride out to the lake if it is as fun as you say."

Not able to stop myself, I burst out laughing, "Samantha!" exclaiming.

Lucas stepped into the kitchen, "We will have to make a schedule with Grayson and Victoria or that spot on the lake could get crowded." He looked at his mate with his eyebrow raised in challenge.

She laughed, then looked up to Grayson, "You need to get Victoria a dress. And convince her to invite her father." As she spoke and walked up to Lucas and stretched up to kiss him, "And am I sure you know of other spots we can go." She whispered and blushed at the same time. Lucas growled low and sensual at her, wrapping his arms around her and kissing her soundly.

Grayson and I left shortly after, that night, I was wrapped up in Grayson's arms. "Should I invite my father?"

Grayson turned his head looking at me, "Why not?" He asked.

Sighing, "I am not sure how to explain what I am now. Or you for that matter."

Nodding he understood, "Your father loves you. And I think he would be disappointed to not be invited."

I agreed, so I called him the next day to invite him. Preparations were being carried out, and guests were arriving. Grayson took me to the airport to meet my father in one of the SUVs. Until I saw him, I had not realized just how much I missed him. "Torie!" He hugged me. I could see out of the corner of my eye, the scowl on Grayson's face. "You are glowing!" my father released me and exclaimed. Then stretching out his hand to Grayson, "You must be taking good care of her then."

Grayson accepted my father's hand. "I am trying my best, sir."

Helping my father get settled in the guest room, I was putting things in the drawers, "Daddy?" I started, then stopped, sighing.

My father came over and took my hand he sat me down on the bed and then sat beside me, "I know, Torie."

"Know?" confused, "Know, what?"

Patting my hand, "That Grayson and now you are different." He was gentle.

"What are you talking about?" I asked again.

Finally, he said with a clear voice, "Lycans, Torie." He patted my hand again, "I know." Then a tear fell from his eye, "He saved your life, and I will be thankful for that for the rest of my life."

Shocked, "But how?" asked, trying to figure out how he could know.

Shrugging his shoulders, "I talked about the day you were hurt. And what I thought I saw, when I asked the guards. They didn't say anything to me directly. But I listened to them talking to each other when they thought I was asleep." He grinned. Then he patted me on the leg, "I would not mention this to your mother though."

Lowering my head, "I didn't even invite her."

He pulled me close, hugging me, "One day, Torrie. You will have to forgive her for leaving us. I have."

"I guess," I whispered to him; I didn't want to think about my mother. She left us so long ago, and I am pretty sure our lives have been better than she hadn't.

Today was the big day, Grayson got up early, and presented me with a large box. Sitting up in bed I opened it, and there is tissue paper was the most exquisite dress I had ever laid my eyes on. "Samantha helped me pick it out." His eyes were on my face.

Gingerly I fingered the tulle and satin when I looked at him, wiping away a tear, "It's beautiful, thank you." I whispered. I pulled out the champagne-colored dress. Lace and tulle formed the capped sleeves, and the bodice was high and flowed out to a loose skirt.

He gently forward lightly kissing me, "You are very welcome." Then he stood and walked toward the bedroom door. "I meet you in the mating circle." Then he was gone for the rest of the day. I didn't have time to think about much all day.

Samantha came over and made me breakfast. Then there was a knock on the door, and when she answered it, she grinned, letting in what looked like an army of people to pamper me for the day. Grayson had arranged for a masseur to come, and then I had a manicure and pedicure. After which I soaked in a tub of hot water with heather sprigs and milk.

Looking out the window from our bedroom, I could see that the sun was setting, and my excitement rose. Taking deep breaths, I chanted. *'Stay down'* to my Lycan within. A hairdresser had put my hair up in an old-fashioned design, with curls pulled free around my face. I sipped on my dress over my head, it was an A-line with a deep V in the bodice as well as the back and stayed in place with a lace belt.

Samantha gasped, "You look lovely!" she said. Then reached out her hand with a gift box, when I opened it there laying on velvet was a tiara with gold and diamond leaves and a teardrop stone that would rest on my forehead, I looked up to her, "From Lord Eryn," she explained. The delivery man came just a few minutes ago." Then she stepped forward, "Let me help you with it." I sat at my dressing table, as she lifted it over my head fitting it through my hair. I felt like a princess.

She looked at the time, and said, "I will see you at the ceremony," Then whispered. "No shoes or..." she paused for a second, "panties."

Smiling I stood and took her advice, I reached under my dress and removed my panties. Then let my dress fall back to the floor. I walked downstairs and then out the back door, there was Samantha's father, kissing my cheek, "I am going to escort you to the mating circle." Patting my hand as he placed it in the crook of his arm. We walked out to the woods, coming to a clearing. I looked up and around to see that there were flowers intertwined in the branches of the trees and torches around. Fergus nodded to my father and kissed my cheek again stepping back.

My father sniffed back tears when he looked at me, "You are so beautiful, Torie." He whispered. Then he looked at Fergus, "He is going to signal me when it is time," explaining. Samantha was standing with little Kelvin in front of her, and on her left was her father, another man that resembled Lucas was on her right, with space in between them. Looking around I only recognized Dr. Herbert standing on the opposite side of the circle. She smiled at me.

A man that looked so much like Grayson came forward from the trees and stopped at the edge of the circle in front of me. He nodded to my father, and Fergus motioned for him to lead me to the center. My nerves were all over the place, and I chanted in my head, *'Stay down'* to my Lycan.

Once I was in place, Lucas came from the trees, holding a torch above his head, he was dressed in black pants, and a crisp white shirt, over which he had a shining breastplate. Though black it glistened in the torchlight. Once he came to the circle, he turned to stand beside Samantha and thrust his torch into the ground. Then each of the others came, Levi, Noah, Wyatt, then Jackson.

I must have been holding my breath because when Grayson came forward, it whooshed out. I thought the others looked nice, but Grayson was magnificent. My eyes didn't leave him as he strode proudly to me, stopping on my right side.

Then his brother, Murdoc spoke I turned my attention to him. Telling of the ancient customs and rituals of Lycans mating. I quickly glanced at my father, seeing that he was wiping a tear away. When Murdoc asked me; "Victoria Marie Campbell do you come here of your own free will to be mated with his Highness, Duke of Arcadia, Grayson Ewan Sinclair?"

"Yes," I said clearly.

Then he stepped toward me offering me his hand, I lifted my dress enough to kneel on all fours, as Samantha told me. Then Murdoc stepped back, speaking to Grayson, "Your Grace, Duke of Arcadia, Grayson Ewan Sinclair, do you agree to protect this she-wolf until the end of your days?"

Grayson boldly said, "Yes." I glanced over my shoulder as his eyes quickly looked into mine.

Murdoc cleared his throat, and spoke again, "You may claim your mate." I tilted my head to the side. I felt Grayson come down and covered my body from behind, first he licked the side of my neck then sat back growling low as his beast came forth, *"MINE!"* His fangs pierced my skin. He licked and sucked any blood that flowed from my neck, then he sat back again on his hunches returning to his human side before he bit me again.

He kissed the side of my neck before he stood and offered me his hand. I barely noticed the resounding howl of our guests around us. I looked up at Grayson, and I felt nothing but pride to be his. But our guests were not going to be ignored, as they all came up to offer us their congratulations, then made their way to Lucas and Samantha's home. Where there was a feast prepared.

Grayson looked down at me and fingered the teardrop from my tiara. I blushed and explained the question I could see in his eyes. "From Lord Eryn."

Grayson nodded, "You are beautiful, Victoria. And you are mine now."

I smiled at his possessiveness, "I was yours the second you caught me on Sinclair Castle."

Growling he leaned down, "Yes you were." Then he looked over his shoulder, "I would like to take you to the lake, but we have guests."

"Does my opinion matter on the subject?" I asked with a grin. He raised an eyebrow and folded his arms across his chest. "I vote for the lake!"

He laughed, and said, "We won't say long at the celebration, then I will take you out to the lake. Okay."

Sighing, "Fine, have it your way."

Chapter 27

Grayson

Victoria and I didn't make it to the lake last night, her father came up to me, and said, "I am going to stay with Wyatt this evening. So, you can Torie can have some private time." Then he grinned and wiggled his eyebrows, patted my arm, and walked away.

When we walked into our bedroom, all I wanted to do was to sink my cock deep into her, and she was very willing. Now I am laying here in our bed with her naked body draped across me, rubbing her back. "What's wrong?" I asked.

"What makes you think anything is wrong?" She answered not looking up at me.

"Victoria," I warned.

She sighed, "Okay. My father." Then she looked up at me, "He is getting older, and I miss him."

I smiled down at her, "Have you talked to him?" at the shake of her head. "Don't you think you should?"

"Boy you have changed!" she giggled, "Before you would have just fixed my problem by growling at him."

Rolling over I let my fangs out, "Do you want me to growl at him?"

Smiling as she ran her hand down my face and lower until she reached my cock between our bodies, "No. Your growls are sexy and only for me." She whispered with a smile.

Lowering my head, I softly growled in her ear, "These growls are for you." She moaned her response as I slipped into her core, and for the next few hours demonstrated my desire for her.

When we finally emerged from our bedroom, it was nearly noon. I went to the kitchen and made coffee and breakfast as Victoria soaked in a hot bath.

That evening, after we ate dinner with my father, I nuzzled her neck softly the way she likes to growl in her ear, then excused myself, and walked out the front door.

Chapter 28

Victoria

Grayson left me blushing after he growled in my ear, I lowered my head to hide my reaction, as my father patted my hand, "You seem happy, Torie? He said with a smile.

Smiling at my father, "Very happy, Daddy," I answered. Then with a sigh, "I want you to move in with us." I just blurted it out.

"Move in with you?" he asked shaking his head, "You are just newly ...whatever." He waved his hand, "I would be in the way."

I thought for a moment, "Maybe we could get you a place in town or build one here on the property." I shrugged, "I have not talked about it that much with Grayson." I admitted. "But I miss you."

He patted my hand, and said, "You talk to Grayson about it." Then he thought, "I don't think having a human hanging around would be a good idea."

I stood somewhat defeated and cleared dinner away and cleaned the kitchen. I was waiting for Grayson on the porch when he came back. As soon as he stepped out, I stood so that he could take my seat, and sat on his lap. "He said no?" He asked seeing my face as he wrapped me in his arms.

Sighing, "Not exactly. Just said he would be in the way here in the house or on the property." Then I looked at him, "Where did you go?"

He laid my head down on his chest, "To see Murdoc." He explained.

"I should have gone with you," I whispered.

Rubbing my back, "He will be here for a week, don't worry." He uttered.

"What am I going to do about daddy?" I asked.

Grayson kissed my forehead, "You are going to respect his wishes, he is your father and your elder."

"Like you respect Murdoc." I assumed.

Another kiss to my forehead, "Murdoc is younger than I am, but he is one of the Princes of Arcadia. So, I show him my respect to a point."

Leaning back, I looked into his eyes. "To a point?" I smiled as he grinned.

Chuckling, "He is still my younger brother. I still can knock him on his arse when training." Then he turned serious, "But I respect his position and title."

Thinking, "If he is younger, why is he the prince and not you?" Then I added, "Are you the oldest?"

"I am the oldest." He answered. "When our grandfathers were chosen to hide the treasure, they had to decide how to have one son become a knight but also be the leader of their clans, and take on their titles of Prince."

I didn't move, as he continued, "Under the advisement of the high council, and Lord Eryn. It was decided that the eldest would train to be a knight, and the second son would inherit the title." He saw the question in my eyes, "If Murdoc does not have any sons, it will be our sons' that will assume the two different roles."

"So your father was an only son, and he only had two sons?" I asked to reason it out.

Nodding. "Correct."

Then I smiled, "What if we only have daughters?"

"Are you trying to tell me something?" he asked laying his hand on my abdomen.

I swatted at his hand, "NO!"

He growled low and sexy, "Then we keep trying. Like we are right now." He stood with me in his arms and took me upstairs to our bedroom. Once I was nude, he tossed me a pillow. "So you don't wake your father. You are loud, mo chara." Then he proceeded to prove his point.

Still worried about my father going home, but I did as Grayson advised, and only brought up the topic with him a couple of times. But he always said the same, he would be on the way here. Then there was the issue of my thesis, I could not very well give it on the treasure now. But I needed my computer, so Grayson took me down to the tunnels to his corridor.

When he flipped on the light, it went back nearly fifty feet, with tables and shelves on the walls, with weapons from all ages. An axe caught my eye, and he explained, "That was my grandfather's"

Then I gingerly fingered the breastplate he had worn to our mating ceremony, "We could open a museum." I uttered.

He laid his hand on mine, "It isn't a good idea to have visitors. Many of these things are extremely old and very valuable. And one day will belong to our young."

Smiling up at him, "You are right." Then an idea popped into my head, "Grayson, do you have a school here?"

Confused, he looked at me, "Just the training for the recruits. Why?" Folding his arms across his chest, he smiled.

I frowned at him, "For our children, especially the girls. Would you not want your daughters ..correction future daughters to be educated?" Then I frowned more, "I am not pregnant." I finished adamantly.

Chuckling, he said, "I know you are not. I would smell it if you were." Then he came forward and wrapped me in his arms, "I had not thought about it. But yes, I think that having our daughters educated would be good, as you said we need to get with the times." Then he kissed me lightly, "What is brewing in your head, Victoria?"

Running my hands up his chest, "I have my bachelor's degree, and I could teach. Then I can resign from my doctorate program." Then I sighed, "But I am going to still have to pay off my student loans. I just can't dump all that debt on my father."

He hugged me close, "I will pay off all your loans, and we will get a house in town, just in case your father changes his mind and wants to live near us. Will that make you happy?"

"Did he say something to you?" I asked against his chest.

Rubbing his hands up and down my back, "No, but I spoke to Lucas and your father is somewhat correct. Having a human living on the compound that isn't a mate, could cause problems."

Leaning back, I looked up into his eyes, "Yes, that would make me happy, thank you." Then I moved away, picked up my laptop, and trailed my fingers over my research notebooks. Smiling, "Let's go home."

The next day Levi spent running internet wires into a guest room, that I had deemed to be my office upstairs. I thanked him by inviting him to dinner, which he declined.

That night laying in Grayson's arms, "Levi seems distant. I mentioned it to Samantha, and she said he is the same way around her.

"We are worried about him," it was a statement of fact. "He has been going out to the woods more and more running with the wild wolves. Our fear is he is going to change and not come back since he had not found his mate yet."

"Then we need to help him with that, make him a part of all of our families." He kissed my head.

"I only wished it worked that way." He mumbled.

Chapter 29

Grayson

Victoria had emailed Stamford University and resigned explaining that she had gotten married and was not going to be finishing her degree or presenting her thesis. Once we had the total amount she owned on her loans, I wired the money to them, paying everything off. I didn't want her to worry about anything.

Within a month after our mating ceremony, she realized she was expecting. She growled at me the first dozen or so times as she ran to the bathroom to throw up. But I had Dr. Herbert come out and examine her. With her now a Lycan but being born a human we didn't know when she would deliver. I stayed close to home as much as I could when she neared her third month since that was normal for a Lycan, but she did not deliver.

Refusing to stop her normal routine of going out to the lake to meditate, about her sixth month along I heard her cry out for me. When I got to her, she was bent over with a heavy contraction, and turned her yellow eyes toward me, growling out in pain. Quickly I picked her up and got her home.

I called Dr. Herbert as soon as I got her up in our bed. Placing towels under Victoria, I held her hand as her contractions got stronger and longer. My sweet mate that barely swore, cussed me to hades and back with each contraction, as her eyes glowed and her fangs elongated. Finally, our son came into the world, Arran Lennox Sinclair. Arran was my father's middle name, and Lennox was Victoria's father's name. But everyone called him Lenny.

Victoria was beautiful, and a wonderful mother. She ordered an infant-carrying sling that wrapped around her and she could place Arran in it and walk around the house. She made plans for a school and continued to research different levels of teaching. She understood that officially she would be home-schooling our children and any future children that were here at the compound. And had started with little Kelvin on his letters and numbers. Samantha would come along and supervise him, even asking Victoria to help her. Explaining that she had not received a formal education, and wanted to learn more.

Lenny came for a long visit, and finally agreed to move into the house we bought for him, just a few miles away from the compound. I had several of the recruits go with him to pack up his house, and made sure it sold for a good price, I never wanted Victoria to worry that he was not financially taken care of.

Though Tavish was still in the back of our minds, he still did not know that the treasure was here, he presumed but thought it was located within the tunnels. It was here, but not where Eryn took Victoria that day, and I suspected that she had looked for it again in the weeks that followed his visit, but she would never find the entrance. It was for the best, I wanted her to be safe.

We receive a message from the high council that Professor Maxwell was dead. I wasn't sure how Victoria was going to take the news, but she just looked at me, and said, "Now we only have to worry about Tavish." Then she walked up to Arran's room and picked him up, holding him close.

Levi was still distant, and we still worried about him, even more so now that Arran was born. That was until Hannah Goldmann showed up at the front gate looking for Levi.

Coming Soon
Levi – Book Four of the Lycan Knights

From K. L. Stephens

Dear Reader,

    I hope you enjoyed Grayson and Victoria's story as much as I did writing it. These characters came to life for me as I brought them to existence for your enjoyment.

    If you loved this book, please leave me a review! I love hearing from my readers.

    The Lycan Knights series does not end here; Wyatt's story will be next. I cannot wait to introduce you to him further. As Wyatt stands outside Auschwitz Concentration Camp, in the winter of 1942 he sees a mother helping her child escape. Refusing to let the child be shot, he intervenes and gets her to safety. Now seventy years have passed, and her granddaughter is searching for the man who saved her grandmother's life.

    Keep watch for Wyatt's story to be released in early 2023.

Thanks for reading,
K. L. Stephens

About the Author

K L Stephens is the author of paranormal and contemporary romances. Her works include The Lycan Knights series, and two novella series The Bennett's and Just Us. Her books have received multiple rave reviews from fans across the globe.

K. L. Stephens loves to take her readers into the worlds she creates as she writes, where she matched her many flawed heroes, to strong women that come to love them despite their shortcomings.

Residing in Southeast, Florida with her spoiled Cocker Spaniel and lazy cat. When she is not working you can usually find her cooking, in the garden of her one-acre home, or reading. Her reading interests are as diverse as her writing. From classic, or sweet romances to spicy paranormal shifters and vampires.

More Books by K. L. Stephens

The Lycan Knights Series
THE PREQUEL
LUCAS
GRAYSON
LEVI (Coming 2023)

Just Us Series
CONNER
HUNTER
DYLAN
EDDIE (Coming 1/1/2023)

The Bennett's
INHERITANCE OF LOVE
INFILTRATION FOR LOVE
INTENSITY TO LOVE
IMPERVIOUS TO LOVE
INSTRUMENT OF LOVE